LOST: A MOUNTAIN MAN RESCUE ROMANCE

J.S. Scott writing as
Lane Parker

Cover Artist: Stacey Chappell
ISBN: 978-1-68-749463-4

Chapter One

James

People say you can judge a man by the company he keeps. His friends, his family, his lovers.

Hell, maybe that old saying *was* true.

If it was, I guess that made *me* a prick because I didn't keep any company *at all*.

And I liked it that way.

Not that I really *cared* what people thought of me. There was nobody who meant enough to me that I gave a damn *what they thought*.

Not anymore.

I'd been in the backwoods for eight years now, and I'd become accustomed to caring only about myself. It was simpler, easier.

I was an artist, a sculptor of wood, and that was the only thing that truly consumed me. I didn't give a fuck about much else.

I stepped outside my secluded, rustic cabin, ready to get back to work after having a sandwich and a beer. As I stretched to loosen up, I noticed that the flat gray clouds were settled on the mountain peaks this afternoon. They edged the snow line like watercolor bleeding on a canvas, while the snow down at my altitude melted a lot quicker in the spring than it did on those soaring mountain peaks. There were rivulets running along the pine-strewn forest floor. It was wet and calm, warm for early spring, but there was a chill *just behind* that warmth.

Perfect day for carving.

Nothing else mattered when I was absorbed with creating something new, and then perfecting it until I was satisfied.

Wood carving had always had a reputation of being a calm, sedate, relaxing craft. But that *relaxing shit* had never worked *for me*.

I made wood *sculptures*; wide, heavy, and solidly *there*. I liked my pieces to *impose* on the spaces they inhabited. I liked them tall, curvaceous, and intimidating.

I put everything I had into my pieces, and I put my *whole body* into the art. I worked fast and furiously, totally *consumed* by my projects, working on them like a frenzied madman.

There was no other way to do it. *Not for me.*

Once I started carving, and the shape and meaning came to me inside the wood, I'd chase that shape like a wolf after an elk. I'd lose all thoughts of the real world, time, and place.

At one time, I'd been what I'd considered a mediocre painter. But not anymore. I'd found what I was *meant to do.* After years of painting flat, one-dimensional pieces, of making the *materials* into *art,* I now found the *art* in the *materials.* Creating my sculptures that way made me forget *everything.*

How I'd gotten here.

Why I'd come.

Why it was necessary for me to be completely alone in the wilderness.

"Shit!" I grumbled, realizing that I'd been contemplating my circumstances way more than usual.

Time to get back to work!

I shook myself out of my morose state of mind,

walked out back, and concentrated on my half-finished carving.

I was lost in the steady scrape and scratch of the chisel against the wood when I heard a shuffle in the forest behind me.

Probably a deer that thinks I'm no threat. The herds liked to snack on the red clover that had just come up after a long winter.

I paused to wipe the sweat from my brow. It wasn't unusual for me to get overheated when I worked for any length of time, so I peeled off the flannel shirt I was wearing.

The shuffling started again behind me, growing louder, closer, and then it abruptly...stopped.

Definitely *not* a deer.

Bambi didn't have *that heavy* of a step.

It sounded more like a lumbering bear.

I didn't turn around. If it *was* a bear, we had an unspoken agreement already. I didn't mess with them, and they didn't bother me. They were black bears and didn't want to be around humans any more than I wanted to be around them. I usually just ignored them, rather than pissing them off.

Could be a hiker.

It was rare for *any* hiker to get up my way, so damn far from Aspen. A few times, I'd spotted backcountry hikers, but those people were on their own spiritual journey. They didn't want to be around people any more than I wanted to be around them.

The intruder finally gained my attention when I heard a very feminine voice curse. "Fuck this."

Yep. *Definitely* not a bear.

It was something worse. A fucking tourist. *A very lost tourist if she's gotten this far off the beaten path.*

What in the hell is she doing here?

I knew I *still shouldn't* turn around. That would make it look like I had some kind of interest in her—which I didn't. The woman could just use her damn cell phone to contact the rangers. *They* could sort her out. It wasn't my job to help stranded tourists who were idiotic enough not to bring a good map.

What kind of tourist veers off their path this far?

Finally, I *did* reluctantly turn around because the curiosity was killing me. I *had* to know what type of woman got herself lost in this wilderness.

Whatever the reason for not just minding my

own business, I found myself looking right at her after I'd spun around.

Holy hell! She was nothing like any tourist I expected to see.

She was still thirty or so feet from the cabin, holding up a creased map in front of her face. All I could really see, other than her bright blue fingernails, was her body and...it was a sight that got me hard almost instantly.

Shit! I really need to get laid.

Even in a thick, down bomber jacket, her curves were very visible—the arc of her hips, the slope of her thighs. I used my imagination for the rest. Being alone, I'd gotten pretty good at being creative with fantasies.

I watched as she folded the map shut, and warm brown eyes suddenly stared back at me.

Holy fuck!

She was...beautiful. A hell of a lot more attractive than my imagination could have conjured up. The woman was obviously from a warmer climate because she had sun-kissed, tanned skin like honey, cocoa colored hair that curled just under her chin, and sweet, full lips that pouted so decadently that I wanted to groan in frustration.

The woman made me think of all the rich desserts I hadn't indulged in for a very long time.

Sweet, but dangerous if a guy were to overindulge.

She blinked a couple of times, making herself look like a spooked deer.

I shook my head a little, wondering if all of my solitude was making me start to fucking hallucinate.

Beautiful women just *did not* walk up to my cabin. They didn't come here *at all.*

Yeah, there were some female art dealers I connected with when I went to Aspen, and I'd taken advantage of their curiosity about the wildness man who preferred to create his art far from civilization. A guy *had* to get laid occasionally instead of getting himself off—which I did most of the time. I'd taken some of those female acquaintances to bed, but that only happened *in town.* Usually in a decent hotel. Whatever I did with those women, with my body, it was really nothing except a brief physical release.

None of them had ever wanted anything beyond one night, and neither had I.

What woman would want to hang out for very long with a freak who lives in this kind of isolation?

I was surprised when the woman who had invaded my privacy kept staring at me. We were kind of like two wild animals sizing each other up, trying to decide who eats whom. I'd happily play the *predator* if it meant running her off, sending her to wherever she was going.

I don't want her here.

She might be one of the sexiest females I'd seen in a very long time, maybe ever. But that didn't mean I wanted her to *hang around.*

"You lost?" I called loudly. My voice echoed, bouncing off the trees, and I put down the chisel I was holding.

Her eyes narrowed, looking at me like I was some kind of idiot. Granted, asking her if she was lost was probably a dumb question. *Of course* she was lost, but I wasn't really asking to *know,* just to *confirm.*

She looked at the woods around us and she sighed so loudly that I could hear it, even from a distance. "Nope. I'm not lost, actually."

I glanced at the crumpled map in her fists and then back to her face. "You sure?" I asked with a frown.

As she moved a little closer, I could see her nostrils flare in agitation as she answered, "Just out for a hike," she said casually. *Too casually.*

I found myself getting annoyed and impatient, which didn't happen very often.

"This isn't even a trail. This is backcountry." I had no clue why I was even talking —she had given me an out and I should have taken it. I could have very easily just shrugged and turned my back on her. I could have been back to work by now. "You shouldn't be out here."

She bit at that full bottom lip. I was pretty sure that the *twinge* I felt while I watched her nibble at that plump, sensual lip had been instinctual, something deep and carnal. I was *almost tempted* to guide her back to wherever she was staying, find the cabin she'd strayed from and... fucking stay for a while. At least long enough to find out if she tasted as good as she looked.

Almost tempted.

But not quite.

Women like her are nothing but trouble, and no matter how badly I want to fuck her, I avoid trouble in any form. Even a form as sexy as hers.

She didn't respond to me. She just reopened her map and scanned it, her eyes worried, even if her comments hadn't revealed a thing.

I released a beleaguered sigh. I supposed that I *could* at least point out where she *should be.* Then she'd be on her way. Far away from *me.* I didn't exactly have neighbors, so she *had* to be pretty far off-track.

"You don't have a cell phone?" I asked in a disgruntled tone.

"Have one. No signal," she answered without looking up from her map.

Shit! Cell phone coverage was spotty in this area, which was one of the reasons I didn't bother having one myself.

I pointed toward a downward slope. "There's a trail down there, and a ranger outpost two miles on. You'll run right into it." I motioned across the valley where it lowered in elevation and was thick with dark trees and boulders. "If no one's there, and they're probably not, there's a call box you can use. You can keep checking your cell phone signal along the way. It might start working as you get down to a lower altitude and that will save you the hike."

She took a deep breath and nodded. Her brow furrowed, and her mouth was tightly set—resolute now that she had a direction to follow.

Stubborn, just like I thought. Which added up to...

trouble. Also... just like I thought.

She started toward the slant of the hill before I could say anything else.

Hell, she has all the information she needs, really.

It wouldn't take her long to get farther down the incline, and over a ridge of short, sharp hills. Then she'd hit the path that would lead her to a trailhead and ranger station. It was a hike, but she had already gotten this far. Although I had no idea how she'd wandered so far off the path, she was certainly capable of finding a ranger station if she'd made it to my cabin.

I went back to my carving. I knew I'd be thinking about her later, when I was alone. But for now, I'd let the lascivious images I had about her fade away. I had no other choice.

"Thank you!" she called from a distance.

I glanced back over my shoulder. She was walking backward toward the trail, her map stuffed under her arm.

She waved and smiled. And something inside me twisted just a little.

Don't thank me. I'm an asshole.

Hell, I hadn't even offered her a ride. But if she was a smart woman, she wouldn't have gotten into a truck with a guy she didn't know out in the middle of nowhere, anyway.

I turned around again, slightly disgusted with myself. A *good* person—hell, a normal person—would go after her. Follow her. Help her. These trails weren't easy once a person went off the main path, and she was lost as it was.

But then, I *wasn't* a good person, and I hadn't been for a long time.

I turned my head to look back at her again, rethinking the way I'd handled the whole encounter, wondering if I *should* have done something different. I had no goddamn idea why I felt some kind of weird compulsion to make sure the woman was safe.

"Fuck!" I cursed as I craned my neck harder to look behind me.

The woman was already gone.

Chapter Two

Keeley

I'd been camping exactly *one time* in my entire life.

I'd been in college, and I'd made a trip to the California desert with some friends.

I'd been cold, bored, and unable to sleep the whole time.

Rocks under my back.

Creepy noises everywhere.

Freezing, even though I was in a sleeping bag.

I'd hated it.

But *this trip* wasn't *supposed to be* about *normal* camping. It was supposed to be about a stunning, Instagram-worthy cabin, all clean lines and glass and comfort, nestled in nature outside Aspen. Surrounded by tall pines and...silence. Complete and utter...*silence.*

I'd just gotten here last night, and I had been so restless this morning, so *not* enjoying the peace and quiet, that I'd gone for a walk.

Just a walk.

A short stroll.

Not a hike.

But I'd gotten so completely distracted that I'd ended up miles from my rental. Maybe I *had* known that I should have been paying attention, but I'd been too busy thinking about *my life.* Which was something I normally *didn't do* because I was far too busy to think about it.

Yasmin did this to me. She talked me into this.

Granted, my friend and co-worker had chosen Central America for her "finding herself" retreat. But were the mountains that different from a retreat in the jungle?

Yep. I was pretty sure that they were...*now.*

Becoming one with nature. This trip was supposed to be *that.* However, I was starting to think it was far more therapeutic to try to find myself in a flatter, warmer atmosphere.

"Instead, I'm miserable and lost. I knew this was a bad idea," I grumbled as I kept tramping through the mountains.

I shouldn't have let myself lose sight of my rental place.

To be honest, the place I'd rented, although beautiful, had scared the hell out of me. I was a city girl. I worked in *Hollywood* for God's sake. I could find my way around in a concrete jungle, but apparently I sucked in the backwoods.

Plus, I definitely wasn't good with silence.

I wasn't okay with being still when all I ever did was chase my own tail in Los Angeles.

I was a production manager in films, and my duties were endless. I made sure things went off without a hitch. Smoothly, and without any drama so we could stay on schedule and on budget.

I was *always* in motion.

I had no idea how to be *still and quiet.*

Actually, just the thought of being alone with all that silence scared the hell out of me.

Which was exactly why I was in this predicament in the first place.

I took a deep breath and let it out. *No time for*

whining. I need to find my way out of here.

And then, I needed to hightail it back to the city where I belonged.

While I'd been lost in the woods, I'd had to contemplate what kind of desperation I'd felt to be out here at all.

At this point, I was afraid I'd be worse off here than I'd been on that miserable college trip.

At least I hadn't been *completely alone* when I'd had a highly uncomfortable night desert camping years ago.

I had a compass, and a map, and could use both reasonably well—at least I'd *thought* that I could. Not that I had much experience, but it had seemed easy enough *at home*.

I slapped aside a tree branch in frustration. *Dammit!* I was an intelligent woman.

So how had I ended up with no clue where I was going? The tall pine trees all kind of looked the same. The rocks and boulders, too.

If that jerk at the cabin gave me bad directions, I swear I'm going to kick his ass.

Well, I would kick his ass...as long as I can find my way back to his place to do it.

"Damn!" My sore feet stepped on loose rocks and sent me skidding. "This place sucks."

Honestly, I knew the altitude was kicking my ass since I lived pretty much at sea level. Technically, it was around two hundred and fifty feet above sea level in the Los Angeles area. So I was basically a flat lander. Sure, I was drinking a ton of water, and I hadn't planned on walking all that far. Especially not during my first day of acclimating to the altitude. Unfortunately, I'd ended up doing a marathon hike at seven or eight thousand feet, which was wearing me out in a hurry.

I stopped, taking a look at the endless expanse of trees and rocks.

Maybe I'd misheard what that guy had said.

I was a little distracted by his face.

After all, it wasn't like I was expecting a gorgeous man to appear out of nowhere. Okay, I *was* stubborn, but the last thing I had wanted to admit to a really hot guy was that I was stupid enough to get lost when I had a map, *and* a compass.

After living in Hollywood for so long, I had an image of what a guy who lives in the backwoods might look like, and it definitely wasn't *him*.

Yeah, he had the requisite mountain man beard, but it had been trimmed up enough that he didn't look like a cult leader of some kind.

He had dark, curly hair that fell to his collar. Thick eyebrows that were furrowed and intense above a strong, straight nose. All that dark hair set off his tanned skin, flushed with work, and his eyes were—blue, and sharp, and dark. I'd had the crazy idea that he could see right through me, which is why I'd avoided looking directly at him as much as possible. Above the beard, his wide, perfect cheekbones had reminded me of a work of art.

When he'd taken off the flannel, his strong arms had flexed and stretched. *Deliciously.* Even at a distance, the fact that he was hard and muscular was perfectly visible. I'd had to force myself to look away from that completely ripped body of his, too.

I cursed and put the sexy wildness guy out of my head because I realized I'd gotten distracted... *again.*

Rocks went sliding under my feet. Bigger ones fell past me, close enough to make me pretty damn nervous. I tripped on a root, barely catching myself before I fell flat on my face.

It sounded like twigs were snapping behind me, around me.

Maybe my idea of the woods was *too Hollywood,*

but it wasn't hard to imagine being followed by some... beast.

But what kind of asshole would send someone into danger like that?

Wait... am I in danger? Umm...no. Not at the moment. If a predator was following me, I would have been dead by now. I shrugged off the whole idea of being in peril and kept walking.

This isn't possible. It can't be. Smart women do not get lost while taking a walk.

Problem was, I was out of my element.

A lot of my friends and coworkers had done this back-to-nature thing to unplug.

Of course, *they* hadn't been *without* their phones for one second while they were doing it, and their social media feeds had been full of artful snaps of roaring fires, and cute little hiking outfits.

"Maybe I would have been better off going to Central America like Yasmin," I grumbled aloud.

My friend's retreat in Costa Rica had helped her enormously. She came back so rested, so relaxed, so moisturized. Better than any spa treatment, she'd said, and the humidity was supposedly so good for her skin.

I'd been *tempted* to do the same destination as

she had.

But really?

Costa Rica, though?

Really far.

Tropical storms.

Big bugs.

No, thanks.

I'd found something a little closer to home. Sufficiently different from my every day in Los Angeles. But not so far that I couldn't run back to Hollywood in case I had a dire emergency at work. After all, my whole life was all about work.

Jesus! I wished I was in Costa Rica *right now.*

I wasn't so sure that I wouldn't rather be lost in a jungle instead of the damn mountains.

Big bugs versus potential mountain lions and bears... The choices were starting to look like a toss-up. Hell, at least I'd *survive* the big bugs, even if they were incredibly disgusting.

As I forced myself to move on, I kept hearing things around me.

Steps?

Movement?

I'm being paranoid. I probably get that way when I'm lost and terrified. Thing was, I didn't usually wander around in the wilderness wondering if I was going to be lunch for a hungry cougar.

"Just relax, Keeley. Go for a hike. Enjoy the silence and give your brain a chance to breathe," I said aloud in a dry tone, thinking about my conversation last night on the phone with my friend, Yasmin, and the shitty advice she'd given me.

Easy for *her to say* from the comfort of civilization, with food delivery and streaming video at her fingertips.

I'd since discovered that the silence wasn't very enjoyable for me. In fact, it was stifling. But fuck knew that I needed some time relaxing *somewhere*. I was worn out. Sucked dry. I worked *all the time*, the city was a grind, the traffic sucked, and I was just... tired.

Tired of all the plastic people in Hollywood.

Tired of running myself into the ground to try and measure up to somebody else's expectations.

Tired of producers and directors taking all the credit for staying within our budget and schedule while I busted my ass to make them look good.

It's not like I was trying to be someone I

wasn't—some eighteen-year-old aspiring actress, or a sixteen-year-old model. For starters, I was twenty-nine, and being in front of the camera was *not* for me. Never had been.

I just wanted to be an *improved version* of myself.

Not so tired.

Not so disillusioned.

Not so...empty.

For example, I'd had a day off a few weeks ago. *One day off.* I'd had no idea what to do with myself.

Do I even have hobbies anymore?

I cursed when I started to imagine I was hearing footsteps...*again.*

I could have sworn that I'd heard pine needles shuffling, and twigs crunching in the trees. I looked around to see if I *should be* really afraid—if there was a bear or coyote out there—

My paranoid thoughts ended when I suddenly tripped over a ridge in the ground. I fell right on my ass and into the dirt.

"If there's a coyote out there watching me, he's got to be laughing by now," I mumbled as I got back on my feet and started brushing the dirt off my jeans.

And then, I saw it.

The trail. I'm on the *damn trail.*

I'd accidentally stumbled onto a tiny, worn path without even noticing.

Unfortunately, my enthusiasm dampened as it dawned on me that it didn't look like the trail I was *supposed* to be on. The path was going *up* the mountain steeply.

The beautiful jerk at the cabin said it would go down.

Okay, so I had a choice to make. Which way? Listen to the jerk and keep moving down, or follow the trail up?

What do I really know about the hot guy from the tiny cabin anyway? For all I know, he could get his kicks by screwing with people. I need to decide what to do myself.

My days were spent making choices for everyone else—budgets, limitations, hires, fires. Generally, I didn't make all that many choices in my personal life.

I *paid* to have everything taken care of for me, because I never had time to take care of myself. The laundry was sent out and sent back. Someone cleaned up all my messes for me. I lived on takeout, which was sad, because I was actually a very good cook. I even had someone to water all my plants.

If I had to keep the plants alive? It would end up being mass murder because of my black thumb.

I was single again, which wasn't a good thing for me at the moment. I hated to admit it, but I felt really...lost.

I'd never wanted to be the girl who *needed* a boyfriend. But I *had* come to depend on my ex. Too much.

He had made all the decisions—choosing what to eat, where to go out, how we spent our valuable free time. Unfortunately, most of our off time was spent on the phone because of our busy careers. *Not intimate. Too busy.* Still, it had been easy for me, as long as I just rolled with it.

Then one day, I just couldn't *roll with it* anymore.

I realized that having everything decided for me wasn't what I really wanted.

That's how I'd ended up *here.* By God, I'd been determined to find my independence.

Find myself.

Figure out what I really wanted from my life.

I'd desperately needed to discover how I could

get back to the old Keeley who existed years ago. The one who liked to read books, indulge in time with friends, and the Keeley who knew how to enjoy a peaceful day reading. And how to make a damn decision without letting someone else decide how my day was going to happen.

So far, my quest for independence hadn't exactly had a great beginning.

But I had a choice *now*. A personal choice.

Go up the trail or go down?

I was going to listen to my own thoughts for a change, like Yasmin had recommended.

I'm taking the trail. Screw that guy. Trails are what I'm supposed to be on, and it's the only damn trail I see right now.

Decision made, I started working my way upward, scrambling around huge rocks, climbing higher, small rocks falling behind me with every big step. After some struggling, I was out of breath. I turned around to see what was behind me *now*. The valley was below, spread out like spiky green Astroturf. Higher up, I could *finally* see the trail I was *actually looking for*, down in a gap in the trees.

Dammit!

I was *really* close to it. *That* certainly made me

feel better. Maybe *I could* find a way out of here, and down to the ranger station. If I was lucky, maybe I'd get a ride with a hot ranger, and rest my aching feet.

I shivered as I heard a low rumble, like faraway thunder.

What. The. Hell.

I knew it wasn't thunder because it started to get louder quickly, and it didn't *stop.*

Dirt and stones started tumbling down from the trail above.

I didn't move. I couldn't. I was too busy trying to process exactly what was happening.

The falling rocks got larger, sharper, and I *still* couldn't go anywhere.

The rumble started to get closer. It *felt* closer.

Suddenly, a jagged slab slid down at me like it was on wheels. I gaped at the earth that was literally *moving.*

I knew I needed to move fast, but I never got the chance.

In a heartbeat, I was on the ground, pain raging up my leg. There was dirt in my mouth and eyes, and stones continued to roll over me, slamming into my ribs and arms.

I felt like I was being buried alive, and I was panicked, but I was helpless, unable to stop what was already in motion.

And then, finally, the rumbling of the earth... stopped.

"Can you hear me?" It was an urgent call that broke through my confusion and pain, a male voice.

I can hear you. I just can't talk because my mouth is full of dirt. Help me. Please help me!

Tears sprang to my stinging eyes as I realized I couldn't speak. All I could do was cough, trying to clear my airway.

"Shit," the voice said gruffly.

I could hear that curse so well that I knew he was close, and I was frustrated that I still couldn't get any words out of my mouth.

I wanted to sob with relief when he crouched down beside me and quickly dug me out of the pile of debris I'd been half-buried in.

"There's more coming down. I've got to get you out of the way, *now*." His voice was calm, but insistent and urgent.

Without another word, he lifted me like I weighed nothing. My head lolled back. My arms were aching, but I wrapped them around his neck anyway.

I needed some kind of anchor. Some kind of safety. And at that moment, the unknown man with an obviously strong body was both of those things for me.

He cradled me protectively, and he moved so fast it was almost frightening.

I heard more rocks coming, that thundering noise that I knew I'd never forget. He was right. The mountain *wasn't* going to stop moving. In fact, it sounded like the whole damn thing was going to topple down on top of us.

My vision started to clear, and I could see that we were moving among the trees like we were on an obstacle course.

My leg hit a low hanging branch as he raced away from the falling rock and debris, and then— *thwack.*

Finally, *some sound* was able to leave my mouth: I let out a *squeal of pain.*

His blue eyes turned down to look at me, sharp and dark.

My brain finally processed *who* exactly was rescuing me.

It's him. Hot guy at the cabin.

Then, everything went black

Chapter Three

James

This is a bad idea. But what in the fuck choice do I have.

I couldn't leave the idiot female to die in a crush of rocks and falling earth.

I kicked a pile of books out of the way and set the woman down on my bed. She was passed out cold. Her shirt was ripped, her jeans were muddy, and there was a bloody stain seeping through the denim at her shin.

Not that I cared whether *my bed* got dirty. But something told me she was the kind of woman who wouldn't be happy about all those stains.

Honestly, she didn't seem like the kind of person who should *be out here at all*.

Hell, what do I know? She was a complete stranger—who was now in *my bed.* And was now *my* problem since I'd just allowed her to break into my solitary state.

I *should have* just tossed her into my truck and dropped her off with the rangers. That rockslide, though...

Never seen one like that in the years I've been here, and I've seen some bad ones. Fucking nightmare scenario.

The rock fall was so close to the road. I kind of had a feeling we were fucked.

We were probably blocked from every road out of the valley.

The only thing there was to do was check the forest service radio and see what they knew.

The woman passed out on my bed could very well need medical attention. Yeah, I could patch up wounds, but what if she needed more than that? She'd definitely gotten beaten up by the rocks during the slide. She could have a concussion, broken ribs, internal injuries.

I growled in frustration.

I turned my radio to the local service frequency. It hissed and crackled while it found the signal, and a tinny voice came through. It was just an automated broadcast, an out-of-date weather report.

I tuned to an open frequency and made a call, reaching out to whoever might be listening. The rangers usually picked up.

Of course, if they were already busy at the rock fall site... *they wouldn't.*

And...they didn't.

All I got was radio silence.

I didn't have a phone here. I never *needed* one, and the possibility of getting a signal sucked in this area, too. No internet service, either. Most of the time it didn't matter much.

Usually, I was alone, and I didn't *need* any help. I didn't *want* any.

I turned to look at the woman. I scowled as I realized she hadn't moved.

Following her had been a bad idea from the start. I hadn't meant to. In fact, I refused to go after her at first. But some damn compulsion had forced my legs to move in the direction she'd gone.

That wasn't the kind of thing I did. Ever.

But the memory of her sweet *thank you* had

turned in me like a knife. I'd been sending her out alone, and lost, and she *thanked me* for it with a wave and the most damn adorable smile I'd ever seen.

I grunted as I looked at her, still shocked that there was anybody in my bed other than...me. *I have no responsibility for anyone except myself.* That was something I had to learn the hard way, years ago. *And yet...*

She hadn't *insisted* that I take her anywhere. The woman was probably stubborn, refusing to depend on someone else, even though she'd actually needed more assistance than she'd asked for when she'd waved goodbye to me.

I knew what *that* was like.

I didn't ask anyone for anything, either.

So I'd followed her out of curiosity, mostly.

Inadvertently, because I was the only one around, I'd probably saved her life. Hell, I was pretty certain *I did.* The woman had been defenseless, like she had no idea what was happening to her. She hadn't even known when to move her ass out of the way of the next slide.

She'd also managed to put herself beneath the road line. Granted, the way out of here for me was more like a two-track. It went up before it went down, and she'd gotten directly beneath the portion that ascended right before it turned into a sharp descent down the mountain.

Actually, it had been a damn good thing that I'd followed her.

However, just because I'd rescued her because I had no choice didn't mean I wanted her *here in my cabin.*

Following her was an aberration. A fluke.

I'd hung back from her as she hiked on down to the valley, just to make sure she found the trail. Then, I'd planned on leaving. I didn't want it to seem like I was... stalking her.

But she just kept veering off the path I had given her.

And then she'd gone *up.*

Why in the hell would a sensible person *do that?*

It was like she wasn't even *paying attention.* Even though her situation was dire, I was pretty sure *she* hadn't known that. I had no idea where her brain had been, but it hadn't been hyper-focused on finding her way back to her accommodations. She'd been wandering around like a city girl who had no idea what kind of danger she'd be in if she couldn't find her way out of the forest before dark.

Okay. I get it. Her thoughts had been somewhere else. No one comes out here alone unless they've got a lot on their mind.

I knew what *that* was like, too.

But *holy hell*, a person couldn't lose themselves in other thoughts when they needed to get back to their cabin before nightfall. And she'd obviously gone far off the beaten path without a single thought to her own safety.

With the big rocks up on the ridge there near the road, and the water from snow melt loosening everything...

She *should have* avoided being under the road line. She *should have* done her research before even walking out into the woods *at all.* She *should have* taken the directions I gave her to keep herself out of a dangerous situation.

She'd made some bad, impulsive decisions.

Like I don't know what it's like to make some shitty choices? She's hurt. Doesn't matter how she got here. Doesn't matter whether the rangers call or not.

Right now, she's bleeding on my bed and out cold.

It didn't take long for me to decide what I had to do, whether I wanted somebody else in my space—or not.

I took off her shoes, and her jacket. Her arms were a map of scrapes and bruises. I lifted up her shirt and spied some nasty contusions on her torso.

The woman was going to be hurting when she woke up. No doubt about it.

The bigger problem was the major gash to her leg, and the fact that she still hadn't moved a muscle. The wound was still bleeding through the denim. Her jeans *had* to come off. *Shit.*

I need a minute to think about that one.

I moved to the bathroom. I rifled through a dusty cabinet for the first aid kit with the bandages and pulled out what I needed.

I scowled as I paused at the edge of the bed.

Jesus! I was *not* the kind of man who takes clothes off unconscious women.

But I wasn't *afraid* to do it. Hell, if she woke up and screamed at me, at least I'd know she was alive and conscious.

I put how damn beautiful she was out of my mind and stripped off my flannel shirt so I didn't get it all bloody. I didn't even look at her as I eased the jeans over her enormous laceration and pulled the denim from her feet.

Well, it's not totally true that I didn't look at anything. I *did* notice something. I looked at *her socks.*

They were thin and bright and unbearably cute—sky blue with white clouds and rainbows. They looked like socks for a little kid, except that written in the clouds was a message that was completely adult: *Up Yours.*

I snorted. *Terrible socks for hiking,* I thought, *but I like the message.*

I tossed a blanket from the bed over her lap and propped her leg up on a pile of pillows.

I shook my head and grimaced as I surveyed the damage the slide had caused. The leg was a mess, a long cut up the shin, but I was pretty sure I could just Steri-Strip the gash together since it wasn't terribly deep, and it would heal. *Thank fuck.* I hadn't done sutures in a *long* time, and I'd only tried it on myself. As a wood carver, I occasionally had accidents, so I'd taught myself how to patch up those injuries without making the drive to Aspen to get them stitched.

I felt around the whole injured area. Her leg didn't appear to be broken, but it must hurt like hell. She flinched and groaned when I started cleaning the wound and then started sealing it up.

"What the fuck is going on?" she mumbled. "Ouch! Dammit! That hurts!"

So much for the female being as sweet as her smile. The angel obviously has fangs.

I wasn't quite sure why that intrigued me, but it did.

She sat up. The woman was a little unsteady, but I let out a sigh of relief that she seemed fairly coherent. Hell, she could yell at me all she wanted if it meant she was going to be awake and alert.

She rubbed her face with her palms and brushed the shaggy brown bangs from her eyes.

Then, she apparently registered who I was, and that I was holding onto her *bare leg.*

"Okay..." She put her hands up, palms facing me. "Where are my pants?"

I sighed. *You try to be nice to someone, and this is what you get—an immediate reaction that I'm somehow trying to hurt her.* I grabbed her jeans in my hand and held them up. "Here. Covered in blood."

She looked down at her shin with a grimace. "Yeah. I kind of remember that." She shuddered. In a calmer tone, she asked, "What, uh, happened, exactly?"

"A rockslide," I said. "Don't you remember?" I put on a final Steri-Strip, let go of her leg and stood up. I left the blood-soaked jeans beside her on the bed and pulled my flannel shirt back on.

I was going to have to talk to her before I could finish the first aid.

"Yeah, but—" She shook her head. "What, is it like an earthquake or something? Did it knock me out? Why was the whole mountain coming at me?"

I shrugged. "Just happens sometimes. That was the biggest rockslide I've seen in... forever. Pretty nasty." I wondered if there was another route clear so I could take her out of here, a back way to get her to some place safe. "And I don't know what happened to make you pass out. It could have been the pain, or the rocks hitting your head. You could have a concussion. But it's a good sign that you're awake now. We'll watch for signs of a concussion."

She rolled her eyes and fell back onto her elbows. It must have hurt, because she groaned again. "Well, I guess I'm just really lucky."

I knew sarcasm when I heard it, but...

"You *are*, actually," I told her flatly. My damn hair kept falling into my face, so I found a hairband in my pocket, yanked it to the back of my head, and secured it.

I used that distraction to process the fact that I was talking to a gorgeous, half-dressed female in my bed, who *shouldn't* be there.

Somehow, I guess I'd counted on her being totally hysterical, but she...wasn't.

She was strange. The woman was annoyingly casual for someone whose life had just been saved.

Didn't she know what could have happened?

"You could have *died*," I stressed. "Why were you even over there? I told you to go down into the valley."

"I had *no idea* where I was going! Your directions *sucked*." Her eyes flashed. They were deep and warm, like chocolate and caramel swirled together.

Her unusual dark eyes narrowed. "Why were you *following* me?"

There it was. I could have *guessed* that she would ask. She might be bad with directions, but she didn't seem stupid.

She had a sharp mind, and it showed in her eyes as she looked at me warily.

Don't ask me why I found that dubious

expression so damn appealing, because I wasn't at all certain why it made the gorgeous female even hotter. Maybe I liked a challenge? Maybe I had a thing for surly females?

I hesitated to reply. The thing was, I didn't *want* to answer that question. I didn't want to get *any deeper* into the bad idea that had turned my brain to mush long enough for me to follow her and rescue her.

I had *done* it; that's all there was to it.

Now I had to live with the fucking consequences.

"You asked for help," I said, knowing I was stretching the truth. All she'd really asked for was...directions. I was the one who had decided she actually needed more, that she needed to be watched.

The displeased scowl on her face would've scared a lesser man. I got the feeling it scared *plenty* of people in her normal life. She was a fierce little thing. No doubt about it. But, fuck me, I kind of liked that about her.

She swung her legs over to sit at the edge of the bed and winced in pain. "No, I specifically *didn't* ask you to *help me.* I didn't *ask* you to come with me. And I definitely didn't ask you to follow me through the woods *like a fucking creeper!*"

I stifled a chuckle. "A fucking creeper who *saved your life.*"

"Yeah, about that," she said. "Why am I *here?*" She motioned wildly to the cabin around us. "Is this some kind of backwoods horror movie situation? Because you know what—I've seen so many slasher films, I think I can get out of this alive."

This time I did laugh. *Hard.* Maybe she *could* save herself. Maybe if I had put on a hockey mask and *chased* her, she'd have found her way to the ranger station, no problem.

"I'm not going to kill you. Promise."

"Easy for you to say. You're not dressed only in a pair of panties and at some mountain man's mercy."

Mountain man? I was a man, and I lived in the mountains. I *guess* it fit. I only thought of myself as *an artist.* Not some eco-warrior, or a prepper waiting on the apocalypse.

How different was I from those men, though? From the outside, I guess it was a distinction without a difference.

Fuck knows what she thinks of this *place,* though. It's bare and quiet. The only things I really kept here were some of my smaller sculptures, a bunch of books, a few old blues records for the turntable, and some postcards I couldn't let go.

Just enough for one person to not go too crazy.

I let out an exasperated breath and finally answered. "You're *here* because you were going in *circles*. You never got all that far from my cabin. It was the closest and only place near the slide."

Her eyes brightened. "If the road is near here, could you take me back to my cabin? Please," she requested, adding that polite word at the end as though it were an afterthought.

I knew what that plea had cost her. She had to be pretty freaked out to ask *me* for anything.

"That could be a problem," I said stoically.

"Why?"

"Road might be blocked by the rock fall. *All roads*. Radio hasn't come in yet, so... I don't know." I shrugged.

Her jaw set tight, she glared at me. Like this was all *my* fault. She spread the blanket, trying to cover her legs.

"Don't." I shook my head. "That cut needs bandaging."

She blinked at me. That spooked deer look

was back in her eyes. "Give me the bandages," she said, reaching her hand out. "I'll take care of it."

It made sense; how uneasy she was. I had never been injured and found myself in the middle of nowhere, with a strange person standing over me. Pants or no pants.

But something in me wanted to let her know she was *safe*.

Something in me needed to let *myself* know I *could* be safe while I was around her.

Since what happened with my sister Olivia nine years ago, since I'd left everyone behind, I wasn't sure I was capable of telling anyone they were safe with me.

Might as well try now. I *brought* her here, after all.

"Let me." The command came out with authority because I was a bossy bastard, but in my throat, it felt almost like a plea.

I knelt at the side of the bed again and settled between her legs, then rolled up the sleeves of my flannel shirt.

"Okay," she said hesitantly. She stared down at me. She looked half-scared, half-aroused.

If she's half as aroused as I am...

I silently chastised myself. Putting a final bandage on her injury was the last damn thing that should be getting my dick hard. Thinking she might *like* me touching her was simply wishful thinking on my part.

My large hand wrapped easily around her ankle, and then my palm slid up the undamaged part of her calf.

I set her foot against my thigh, and I could feel her warm skin, even through the sturdy denim material of my jeans. The heat from her body met mine. The old bedsprings squeaked when her hands grabbed onto the mattress. I didn't know exactly why she felt the need to hang onto something so tightly.

Pain, probably.

There was an urge in me to softly stroke her skin with my rough fingers.

I had a *deeper* urge to do *a lot more*. I wanted to lean forward and run my hands farther up her leg. I wanted to find out how sweet her lips really were.

Son of a bitch! It was almost impossible to curb the beast inside me that just needed to touch her.

However, I didn't do any of the things my body was urging me to do.

Instead, I took a breath and kept my hands steady.

She flinched when I put the clean gauze pad against her cut. "Still hurts?"

She grunted softly. "It's getting better. I think. Honestly, my entire body feels like I got run over by a truck."

"You're bruised up. So it's no surprise that you hurt everywhere."

No one wants to admit it when they're hurt. Even when it's obvious.

I wrapped her leg in the bandage slowly and pressed the pad tight.

She was quiet; so was I. After all, we were complete strangers. I had no idea what to say to her. I hadn't exactly had all that many conversations with anybody over the last eight years or so.

Finally, she broke the silence. "What's your name?" Her voice wavered a little.

I really didn't want her to know my name. It made things too damn personal. But I was already doing things I would never do. "James."

"Thank you, James. For rescuing me."

I grunted in response. Nobody thanked me for

LOST: A MOUNTAIN MAN RESCUE ROMANCE 47

anything, so I wasn't sure how to respond, so I asked, "And just who did I rescue?"

I didn't want to know her name, either. But I *had* to know.

She huffed a nervous laugh. "Keeley Norton."

I looked up at her. Her dark eyes were sparkling, her cheeks flushed pink.

It was doing something to me...

Something I wanted? *Oh, hell, yeah.* But it wasn't a good idea.

It was hard for me to take my hand from her leg. But I did. The bandage was all taped up and finished.

"Well, Keeley, this is my cabin. I hope you don't stay too long," I grumbled honestly.

"Let's hope." She smiled, like I was joking.

Honey, I'm dead serious.

She was giving me that sweet smile again, the one she'd given me before the rockslide.

Her guileless, cheerful demeanor had been like a stab to my gut with a very large knife.

Really, maybe *that* was the real reason I'd followed her. After all, nobody had been nice to me in a long time.

That same pain twisted into me again, but this time it was a little bit different. *Softer, brighter.*

I didn't have enough time to think about how I felt about that, even if I'd wanted to. There was a static buzz and pop from the radio.

"White River Dispatch, FA1VV, foxtrot alpha one victor victor, you still on this channel? Got big problems your way."

Chapter Four

Keeley

So this *wasn't* what I'd expected from *hot mountain guy*. Actually, I'd never thought I'd see him again. *At all.*

However, the handsome jerk who had given me bad directions had actually *saved my life.* Not only that, but he'd cleaned and bandaged my leg.

But the biggest surprise had been when he'd *looked* at me like he couldn't decide whether to dump me back outside his cabin or fuck me until we were both completely satisfied.

His eyes were so intense. They were cold blue, like a frozen pond, but they occasionally *burned.*

And so do I. Every time he gives me that heated stare.

Okay. *Most of the time,* he made me feel like an unwanted guest, but he had been brave enough to walk right into a potential death trap and carry me out of it.

Maybe he wasn't such a jerk, after all.

I pulled my legs onto the bed and covered them with the blanket.

He hurried to the radio, which had started to hiss loudly.

"FA1VV, FA1VV, this is ADT2B, alpha delta tango two bravo." He held the microphone in his wide hand. *The one that was just around my ankle.* "Just SE of Baxter and there's a rock fall down from the road line."

"ADT2B, copy that, we heard. You okay?" A woman's voice, business-like, came through the speaker.

"Kind of." He glanced back at me. There was almost a smile on his face, which surprised me. I didn't think he was capable of turning up those sexy lips at all.

James was the brooding type. *Gruff. Ornery. Dark and mysterious.* Not to typecast him, but he fit the call sheet for that type of guy.

I heard the woman's stern voice again. *"Well,*

make sure you are, 'cause there's no throughway until we get this mess cleared."

"None at all?" he grumbled.

"Nope. Backways up near CB are flooded with melt, and I don't think you'd get to those anyway. How many KM from Baxter?"

"'Bout five."

"Pretty isolated. Sit tight, they're gonna get the fall off the road in about forty-eight."

He sighed. "Roger that. Thank you."

I didn't understand what was said *literally*, but I got the gist. Even if I hadn't, I would have *guessed* by the way he slammed his hands down on the battered desk, and his back tensed.

"So, uh, bad news?" I asked hesitantly, as though the truth wasn't pretty damn obvious.

"Road's blocked." He didn't turn around. "No way to get out for two days. At least."

Two days. I was sure that couldn't be right. Like I knew anything about it, but... *two days?!*

"But, um..." I didn't really know to say it without sounding demanding. So I put on my clearest, take-no-shit voice, the one I use for producers who weren't great at listening. "You *have* to get me back to my cabin."

He turned around then, and I wished he hadn't. He looked at me, hard. It wasn't the look from earlier that felt so good.

Not at all.

The man's expression was grim.

"First of all, I don't *have* to do anything." He shook his head and looked away, clearly frustrated. "Second, I don't know how to tell you any clearer. We're stuck here."

Stuck. The word bounced around in my head like a pinball. In my world, there was no *stuck.* There was *always* a fix.

But considering this *wasn't* my world, I *had* to rely on him. I *had* to convince him.

"I can't stay here!" I grabbed the blanket and tried to stand, but pain shot up my leg. I fell back onto the bed, grabbing my shin. I was sure I looked like an idiot, but I didn't care at the moment.

"I don't even *know* you," I pleaded. "Look, you totally saved my life. Thank you. I owe you, like, *a lot.* But I *can't fucking stay here!*"

His jaw worked while he stared back at me. There were probably a hundred things he could have said to me. Ninety-nine of them probably involved serious insults.

Kudos to him for keeping that on lockdown. I sure can't.

"Listen to me... I don't like it, either," he said. "*At all.* I don't *want* you here. No offense." That last part was more than a little sarcastic.

So I rolled my eyes at him and threw it right back. "None taken."

"But I'm not gonna *carry* you all the way back to your cabin. If you could even *find* it."

That was low. He *was* still a jerk.

I folded my arms across my chest. *This is ridiculous.*

This is why I never should have left the Los Angeles metropolitan area. I was so far out of my element that my usual confidence in my abilities was nearly nonexistent.

"So, now what?" My teeth were grinding against each other.

"So," he said, stuffing one of his errant loose curls back into confinement, "*you* can sit your ass right there. *I'm* going back to work. I'm not on vacation."

Just like that, he didn't care about me at all.

The guy who had gently bandaged my wound was completely gone, replaced by a darker, more selfish type of man.

His eye color had morphed into a very chilly ice-blue, and they were emotionless.

He paused at the door and pointed to a dresser near the bed. "There are some pants in that bottom drawer. Too big for you, but at least you'll have something."

The door creaked open and he disappeared past it, letting it slam behind him.

"Wait!"

He didn't wait.

"You want me to sleep... *here?*" I mumbled, looking around nervously.

The cabin was all one room, plus something that might be a bathroom. Open kitchen, if by that you meant beat up counters and a rusty stovetop that *should* have been hidden away. Dusty bookshelves. A lumpy-looking, threadbare couch.

This place was *not* going on Instagram!

James could live however he wanted to live. I wasn't judging. Well, not much. It was just kind of funny—*he* was every bit the mountain fantasy, but this place was *nowhere near it.*

And what is his work, *anyway?* I peered through a dusty window and found him in the back yard.

He was bent over a table, strapping on a pair of safety glasses and scratching his beard. He lifted up something large, and metal, and very sharp-looking.

I was really trying to take his word for it that he wasn't some kind of backwoods killer, but whatever he was holding sure as hell looked like a murder weapon.

I lay back on the bed and sighed before panic hit me. *My bag, my stuff. Where is it?*

I looked from left to right before I spotted the purple strap of my backpack beside the bed, and the fuzzy pink keychain attached to it. It definitely stood out among all that... *brown.*

I reached out and pulled my backpack onto the mattress, rifling through it quickly. I found my wallet, my keys, my phone, an extra hoodie, and a pair of shorts. All the important things. Including a few good sheet masks for my face.

Hey, I *was* trying to relax, after all. Although, I must have been brain dead when I'd tossed them into a *hiking* backpack.

My phone was half-charged, and I opened the settings to check for wi-fi. I should have known— nothing. *Of course* there was no signal.

Who lives like this? Does he even have a plug for me to charge my phone?

Does he have electricity? Plumbing?

I let out a frustrated sigh of resignation. It was no use. I really *was* stuck with the surly asshole who may or may not be a serial killer.

I started to think that maybe if I closed my eyes for a while, I would wake up back in my glossy, clean cabin. I would be in soft bamboo sheets, an essential oil diffuser beside the bed. Then I could wash the day away, use one of those sheet masks, and make one more attempt to enjoy the silence.

There were no bamboo sheets in *this* cabin. But the bed was comfortably scratchy, and warm. It smelled like fresh pine, like campfires.

Like...him.

I felt worn out, and beaten up, my entire body aching from every rock that had pounded into me during the slide.

I closed my eyes, allowing my mind to rest.

After a few moments, I was asleep.

***

When I woke up, chilly and sore, it was already dark outside.

There *were* lights on in the cabin. *So he does have electricity, small mercies.* The lights were dim and soft, small lanterns and lamps. The corners of the cabin were dark.

I could hear water running, so the place obviously had plumbing of some kind. Someone was taking a shower. I really hoped it was James, and not some creepy roommate he failed to mention. *Or a bear he keeps as a pet.*

I got up slowly and reached for the drawer he told me about. I yanked out a pair of black sweatpants.

These are fine. I am not interested in going through a strange man's drawers.

I pulled them on, minding my bandages, and pulled the waist cord as tight as it could go. They still sunk to my hips.

I knew James was a... large guy. Tall, and broad. *That,* I couldn't miss. Obviously, I hadn't known precisely *how* large until now.

It made me more than a little nervous to be cooped up with him, but deep down, I was also thankful. Grateful he had been kind to me during some of the short time we'd spent together. *Kind* being very relative.

Yes, he *was* a jerk, but he *had* helped me. He saved me. He hadn't done anything to me that even hinted at something... truly frightening.

Someone else, someone with nastier intentions and less scruples, could have found me, right?

If there was anyone else out there in the woods.

That thought made me nervous, too.

Pretty isolated, the woman on the radio had said.

Why do you live like this, James? Out here, all alone?

The pressure in my leg stung, but it didn't make me want to squeal *ouch-ouch-help-me*. Definitely an improvement.

I pulled the sweatpants up and reached for my hoodie. It was getting a little colder in the cabin now that it was dark.

I limped around, putting most of my weight on my good leg, and took a longer look around the cabin.

Over the old wooden desk with the radio, there was a large map, better than the one I had. I moved closer to look at it.

Clearer routes, even I could see that. The hiking paths were marked with little flags, and handwritten notes. One read: *beautiful area - hawk's nest.* Another said: *sunset here is unreal.* The tags on various areas went on and on, and I had to wonder whether those brief notes on the map had been written while he was first exploring the area.

I noticed that there were *lots of notes* that just had one short word: *wood.*

Wood. There was a ton of wood around the cabin. Not just outside—inside, too. Even for a cabin in the middle of the forest, it seemed like *a lot.*

There were carvings on the desk, on the shelves. The smaller ones were about the length of my forearm. They sat on round bases and stretched and spun upward, in spirals and strange shapes. Smooth curves were polished to a gleam. The woodgrain seemed to match the shape they took.

All of them were unique. Like little totems to some spirit I had never heard of.

A taller version stood in a corner, just shorter than I was, near a bookshelf stuffed with well-read books. It seemed like it was reaching up, like a living thing. Like a tree still growing. The wood seemed to glow, even in the dim light.

I went and rested my hand on it, marveling over the fact that it still felt...alive. Obviously, it was an illusion. It didn't look like it was still capable of growing, but my heart beat a little faster as I ran my hand over the surface, staring at the way the lines and swirls somehow spoke to me.

It was beautiful. Breathtaking, really.

The door opened behind me and I turned.

James had come out of the shower wearing a faded blue towel wrapped around his waist, and nothing else.

My heart tripped, and I knew I was gawking at him, but I couldn't look away.

Up close, the guy was stunning. Just as gorgeous as the sculpture.

There was a dusting of dark curls all over his broad chest, and they trailed down his stomach. Water glistened in the soft lines of muscle along his torso. His tanned skin was warm and flushed from the heat of the shower.

His wavy, wet hair dripped onto the round muscles of his shoulders, and his arms flexed as he tried to keep the towel wrapped tight.

Too tight, really, to hide the outline of a significant endowment.

I couldn't look away. Whether he was a jerk, or my hero, or both—whatever he was, he was *so damn gorgeous.*

His brow furrowed, and for a moment I thought I saw a blush across those model-perfect cheeks.

"Sorry," he muttered. "I, uh... just a habit. I'll—"

"It's fine." I actually squeaked. I forced myself to turn back to his shelves. *Oh, how fascinating, what excellent books,* I thought, *much more interesting than a wet, naked man.* The flush on *my* face was definitely real, and it took a hell of a lot to make me blush.

I heard him shuffle behind me. I was embarrassed to admit, even to myself, that I wanted to remember what he looked like. And that I would think about it later. Much later.

"All right," he said roughly, his embarrassed tone gone.

I almost didn't want to turn around, but I did.

He was dressed, though, and that was best for everyone. In another flannel. It had to be the uniform out here.

But the gray sweatpants weren't doing a much better job than the towel at hiding anything.

I jerked my eyes away from his groin.

For God's sake, don't think about that.

Chapter Five

Keeley

James made me dinner. Well, if you could call it that.

Ham sandwiches and beer. I didn't want to be picky. It was a decent beer, and really *anything* was welcome at that point.

The sandwiches, though?

Strictly college food.

And that was okay. I was a takeout queen—I could hardly criticize. It had been *way* too long since I cooked something good. Something for myself. If I could just get a little more time in my day... which was probably impossible.

I looked around at his kitchen while we ate. The counters were clear, the stove *looked* functional. It was decent enough, the closer I got.

I could work with it, if it came to that. And I really hoped it *wouldn't* come to that, but it seemed like I was stuck here.

He sat across from me at his table. It was... *rustic*, I guess. It looked like he'd stolen it from a picnic area. He chewed his sandwich quietly, looking anywhere but at me.

I figured he probably felt pretty awkward, having someone just land in his lap like this. Especially someone like me. I hadn't been the most gracious guest so far.

Also, I nearly saw him naked, so there was *that*, too. I couldn't stop thinking about it. I had to wonder what was going on in *his* head. Unfortunately, I'd discovered that James wasn't much of a talker.

I took a swig of beer. "Thanks. For dinner." I held up what was left of my sandwich.

He shrugged. "I don't have guests. Or cook. So..." He seemed apologetic. For *him*, anyway.

"No, it's good. You don't cook for yourself?" Out here it seemed like if you didn't cook, you didn't get to eat.

The area wasn't exactly crowded with

restaurants.

Forget delivery.

"I just eat when I need to. Don't really think about it, otherwise." He took a big bite of his sandwich.

Oh, God. One of those people. Can't relate. I love my food, even if it is takeout. "I like to cook. I just wish I had more time for it," I answered wistfully.

He looked at me for a minute, confused, like he wanted to say something, but he didn't want to *say* it. "What, uh... why don't you have time?"

Now *I* was confused. Was this an attempt at human conversation?

If so, I would take it.

"I work in film production." When he stared at me blankly, I didn't know what to do. "Movies and TV."

He rolled his eyes. "I know what film production is. I just..." He shook his head at me and chuckled. It was like I'd said I jumped on a pogo stick for a living. Which was kind of an apt metaphor.

"Is that weird to you?" I asked.

"No." He took a long drink and looked at

me over the bottle. "Well, yeah, to *me* it's weird. Being around so many people. Making fake things all day."

Now *that* was a criticism I hadn't heard in a while. It was always these artsy guys who said it. Working in Hollywood was low art, if it was art at all. They had no idea.

"Fake is pretty subjective," I replied. "For example, all those novels you have on your shelf are fake. Fiction. It's all expression. It all elicits feelings. Right?"

He nodded in acknowledgment. "True enough." There was a hint of a smile pulling at the corner of his mouth. "Keep you pretty busy?"

Busy. It was a never-ending parade of demands and dumpster fires. I remembered when it was fun, but that was years ago. "Constantly. I'm pretty sick of it. I guess... I wanted to get away from it for a while."

He looked at me, his brow tensed. I didn't know what he was thinking. Part of me didn't care. I wasn't here to justify my life to him.

I wasn't here in his cabin for any reason now, except to wait until I could leave. *Shit.*

"Sorry you got hurt." He brushed the long, loose hair back behind his ears. "Doing okay?"

Somehow he had the ability to be human one moment, a grumpy robot the next, and jumped between the two at will.

I liked the human side. Maybe a little too much.

"I am. Thanks." I smiled at him.

What if the human side just needed a little encouragement?

I wondered what happened to him. Something must have *happened*. That's how most of these mountain man stories always go, right? Of course, that's not the kind of thing you just *ask*.

He drained the last of his beer, and then went to open the ancient fridge in the corner. "Shit. No more," he grumbled. He let the door fall shut and turned to face me. "Whiskey?"

"Huh?"

"Do you like whiskey? Do you want some?" That almost-smile was back. Maybe the encouragement was working.

However, I wasn't sure how much I wanted to drink at the moment. My nerves were still shot, I had no clue where I was, or when I would really get home, and my leg was still throbbing, despite the ibuprofen James had given me before dinner.

"You know, you're not supposed to drink liquor after beer," I informed him.

He smirked at me, his eyes dark blue now, and sparkling mischievously. It hadn't escaped my notice that it looked good on him. "One beer. I think we'll live."

That smirk sent a very *different* throb through me. I hated the fact that I couldn't stop my physical reaction to this man. One look, and heat flowed between my thighs, and my body hummed with a need that was completely foreign to me.

He turned to one of the cabinets and rummaged through the bottles. I supposed there were worse ways to spend a night than drinking whiskey with a devastatingly attractive man.

It's not like there was anything *else* to do.

I'd already concluded that if he was a serial killer, he would have offed me by now.

When he returned with two shot glasses, I took one and sipped it. The whiskey bit at my tongue, sharp and sweet.

James tossed his back in one gulp and smirked again.

Well, I always *hated* to be outdone. I drained my glass, smacked it down on the table, and shot him a satisfied smile of my own.

I got a laugh out of him. A short, guarded laugh. But I would take it. Even if it did sound rusty, like he hadn't made that sound in a very long time.

A couple more glasses, and the night *did* go by faster. We drifted toward the bookshelves, and I ran my fingers over one of the small totems.

"So... you made all these?" There were so many of them, in so many variations, I figured they *must* be his.

He simply nodded.

I turned one over in my hands, and I could feel him watching me, almost like he was nervous about how I felt about his work.

Honestly, I'd only seen a piece from one of his equals—once. Several years ago. James's sculptures were superb, and it wasn't just his technique. It was his ability to make the wood come to life.

I smoothed my hand over the piece I was holding, marveling over the perceived warmth of the carving.

"I saw something like this several years ago at an art exhibit," I mused aloud. "I'd desperately wanted to buy it, but it was way out of my price range." I was putting it mildly. The beautiful carving had been tens of thousand of dollars. And when I'd gone back to see it one more time before leaving the exhibit, it had already sold.

"In Los Angeles?" he asked huskily.

I nodded absently. "I wasn't even allowed to touch it unless I was ready to buy."

"You can have that one," he said gruffly. "Touch it all you want."

I shook my head regretfully. "I can't take it unless you let me pay for it. It's a beautiful work of art. How much do you charge for your work?"

He shrugged. "Not an issue since it's mine to give. Take it. I have a ton of them around, as you can see."

I carefully put the carving back. "Your work is just as good as that piece I saw at the exhibit," I replied. "I can't take it. But thank you for offering."

"I insist," he persisted. "Take it when you...go."

"We'll see," I said vaguely, knowing I'd never take something that incredible without paying for it. It was obvious he put his entire soul into his creations. "They're all amazing. Every sculpture. Tell me about them."

He scratched the back of his neck, and he *almost* seemed bashful. The blue of his eyes darkened and glittered when he told me about his process, how he found the shapes in the wood.

James was *magnetic* when he talked about his craft. I hadn't even realized my hand was on his arm as I listened to him, until I stumbled. My foot caught on a knot of wood in the floor, and I fell forward, but he was already there to catch me.

His arms wrapped around me and pulled me close. He was warm, and he smelled like his bed—pine and fire and something deeper, wilder. I gripped his arm and looked up at him.

"Sorry," I mumbled.

Lips parted, he stared at me. It felt like he stared *into* me.

"Better sit down," he said. His arms still holding me close, he guided me to that old couch in the corner. I limped along beside him and fell onto the cushions.

He sat next to me. Not so close he was touching me, but close enough that his masculine scent still tormented me.

We sat and didn't speak. The cabin was quiet. The only thing I could hear was an owl, hooting faintly, far away.

The quiet settled my mind. Strangely, I realized that it was the kind of quiet I'd been looking for. Not glass-encased silence, like the cabin I had booked, but something more *natural*.

Those thoughts surprised me. I wasn't sure what it meant that I was enjoying the silence. I fiddled with the drawstring of my pants—his pants—and filed it away to think about later. Just like I'd put aside the way he'd looked when he walked out of that bathroom in nothing except a towel.

"Why are you out here alone, Keeley?" he questioned huskily.

His voice startled me out of my thoughts. I felt his sharp eyes staring at me. I supposed he was going to ask eventually. Whether I *wanted* him to ask was another matter.

The thing was, I knew why I'd come to Colorado. The answer just felt stupid when I put it into words. I was out here alone to prove that I could be. I wanted to find out if I could be alone and not succumb to all the anxiety, to my nervous, rattling brain. I wanted to do something for myself, to make choices for me.

I wanted to find out who I was, and why I felt so alone.

Talk about first-world problems. I needed to go on a vacation to take care of myself—for once. Not exactly a worldwide, serious issue.

Wait. Did he *really* mean, *why are you out here alone? No friends? No boyfriend?*

Yeah, I *had* friends. I had friends like Yasmin, who gave me advice I didn't want to take, though she meant well. I didn't have close friends, deep conversation friends, emotional support friends. I was always going. I didn't have *time* to think or feel.

Some part of me didn't even *want* to do those things.

Which was probably a big part of why I didn't have a boyfriend anymore.

Well, I wasn't going to tell *James* any of that.

I sighed. "I guess I'm still figuring that out. What about you?"

Fair's fair, after all.

He shrugged and brushed his hair behind his ears. "Long story." His voice was clipped and closed-up. It was the kind of tone that said—*don't ask any more.*

But the whiskey in me said—*go for it.*

"We've got nothing but time," I said.

He shook his head. "Let's just say I'm a sorry bastard who probably needs to be alone."

He didn't say it with self-pity. He said it with resignation. A sorry bastard was what he was because he had decided that was who he wanted to be.

The problem was, the more I talked to him, the more I got the feeling that *wasn't* who he was at all.

James was passionate and interesting and, yeah, maybe a *little* strange. *Definitely* prickly. Stubborn. And kind when he wanted to be. Admittedly, he wasn't exactly warm and fuzzy, but he was far from being what I'd consider a *total* asshole.

Maybe I just knew too many *real* bastards, people who wouldn't lift a *finger* if you were in trouble, to lump him in with *them*.

"Damn, it can't be *that bad*," I coaxed. "You didn't kill anyone, did you?" I laughed, but he... didn't. His brow wrinkled and he looked down at the whiskey glass in his hand.

Oh God, he killed someone? I didn't want to be right about that.

"No." He looked into my eyes. His own were deep, and dark, and troubled. "But it's not worth getting into."

Okay, time to put that shit out of your mind, Keeley. He's fine. Remember? If he wanted to kill you, you'd probably be toast by now.

Stop thinking about that.

"Well," I said, "you make beautiful art out here. So it seems like it's working out. If you're going to be a misanthropic loner, might as well make the most of it, right?"

He smiled. "That's what I've always thought."

His smile was so... good. It shouldn't have been, but it was. It felt like a rare sight, something you shouldn't have seen, like a wild predator chasing a butterfly. Or something.

Okay, the whiskey has definitely hit me.

The way his strong jaw moved, the way his eyes lingered on me, and seemed to search my face, and settle on my lips... That hit me, too. Not in my brain, but in my belly, between my thighs, low and hot.

"What I meant earlier..." His gaze fell to my neck as he spoke, and my skin grew hot as he looked at me. "It's hard to believe there isn't someone... someone who didn't want you to come out here alone."

He snapped his eyes up to mine then, and they burned into me. He didn't say a word, but he'd spoken loud and clear.

Let me know you want me. Tell me. Say it. Tell me that there is no one else.

So I did.

"Well, I'm not alone now." My hand drifted toward his leg. My fingers stretched across his upper leg, and I felt the hard muscle of his thigh beneath. "Neither are you."

The whiskey I'd swilled down made me bold, and brazen, stripping away any inhibitions I might have had over approaching James like some guy I was trying to pick up in a bar.

His nostrils flared, but his eyes didn't leave mine. He pulled my hand from his leg forcefully and raised it to his mouth.

His beard brushed against my palm and I shivered. His lips touched my skin, and his tongue licked up my hand, across the skin between my fingers. I squeezed my thighs together. The pounding throb thundered into my brain. He sucked one of my fingertips into his mouth.

Is this really what I want? I'd started it. I couldn't deny that.

He leaned closer, my hand still in his. He pinned my arm above my head, against the arm of the couch. His weight pressed me into the cushions, his body hard and hot. His free hand stroked up my leg, my thigh. I wanted to spread my legs around him, *desperately*. But they were stuck beneath him—I was stuck beneath him. Even that felt *so damn good.*

He brushed his lips against my neck, and I felt his tongue on my skin. His kisses were open and wet. Then his teeth grazed my throat. A choked moan escaped me, and I couldn't hold it back even if I wanted to.

Yes. This is what I wanted. I wanted *him.*

James left me needy, raw and wide open to him, a feeling that was as scary as it was seductive.

I'd never experienced this kind of wild desire, but dammit, I wanted to indulge in the sensations.

I'd wanted James since I'd seen him outside, sweaty and irritated and fucking gorgeous. And when he was on the floor, my leg in his hand while he bandaged me up, I hadn't been able to think about anything else. Even if this was a mistake... it was going to be a delicious one that I could never completely regret.

"You okay, Keeley?" he asked tightly. "Your

injuries—"

"I'm fine," I panted. "Please don't stop."

He kissed up my throat, over my jaw, but when he reached my mouth, he stopped. His hand stroked up my side, and his fingers found my lips, tracing them. I could only watch, my skin burning, as his eyes searched my face, like he wanted to remember every part of it.

I fell into the heat of his gaze, mesmerized, my heart stuttering as he looked at me like he was trying to commit everything about me to his memory. The action was unbearably sexy, and it left me breathless.

Before I knew it, his lips were on mine, hard and wanting. His teeth bit at my bottom lip and tugged. I opened my mouth the way I wished my legs could open around him and jerk his hard body against mine.

Our tongues touched, and a low growl rumbled through him.

He clawed at my shirt and grasped my hip. Rough fingers dipped under the loose waistband of my pants, and I moaned into his mouth when they moved inward. He pressed into my thigh and brushed between my legs.

"Fuck." He groaned and pulled his hand away.

I could feel his breath hot against my chest. He pushed my legs open. I gasped at the feel of his rough fingers cupping me, spreading me.

James was real, and he was earthy. His hands weren't manicured or smooth. He was rough, but it was one of the things that made him almost irresistible. When he was fucking a woman, none of it would be practiced, nor would it follow some kind of technique.

It would be raw and feral, and his unbridled need would turn my desire into something just like his.

I squirmed as he bit softly at my nipple through my shirt. I writhed beneath him, whining.

"You are so wet," he whispered. "And right now, you're mine, Keeley." He pressed one of his thick fingers inside me, and I clenched, shaking. *Jesus!* I *was* his, and I sure as hell wasn't about to argue about that. I responded to his every touch, his every word, his every breath. The fact that he'd stated that he owned my body, and had uttered it so damn possessively was like an aphrodisiac to me.

I looked into his eyes, and they were darker than ever, nearly black, and sparkling dangerously. His finger thrust over and over, and his eyes never left mine.

"I bet you taste as sweet as honey, Keeley," he rasped.

Just the thought of his slick, hot tongue devouring me made my body jerk.

My head rolled back, and his thumb moved up, circling my clit. I bucked against him. *I could come like this, right now. Please don't stop. Pleasepleaseplease—*

I cried out as I reached my climax, and everything went dark as I squeezed my eyes shut, my body rigid and thrusting against him. I gripped his flannel shirt in my fists while he held me, and my panting slowed.

My eyes were still closed, and I waited for him to move. I waited for him to do more, to press his body against mine. To take me like I belonged to him.

Greedily.

Covetously.

Hard and hot.

Instead, I felt myself being lifted from the couch. He carried me with ease, just like he'd done at the rockslide, and he set me down on his bed. He reached for the crumpled pile of covers at the foot of the bed and pulled them over me.

"I loved watching you come for me," he said hoarsely.

He didn't lean down on the bed, and he didn't touch me again. He only sighed, his brow tensed, and turned away.

I reached for his shirt again. "Wait. Don't you want—"

"No." That clipped tone was back, the one that said—*stop*. "I shouldn't have done that, but I couldn't stop myself."

"But I—" I didn't know how to say it. I liked it? I wanted more? Yeah, all that, but also... *why shouldn't you have done it?*

We were grown adults. We wanted each other. Hell, I more than wanted him. My body was screaming that I *needed* him.

He turned off the lights near the bookshelves. "Listen... It isn't you. You're—"

He ran a nervous hand through his thick, wavy hair. "You're beautiful, and you're hurt. And you deserve better than a drunken fuck with someone who's hardly a person anymore."

What? I rubbed my eyes. Confusion was making a mess of my brain. If I had been a little less bewildered and a little more sober, I would have felt pretty awful about myself. Insulted *and* injured.

Instead, I just felt thrown off balance. He was right—it *wasn't* me. It *was* him. He was like a feral cat swatting wildly, because he didn't know how to accept an affectionate caress.

For all the grown-up woman advice I'd ignored over the years, one thing really had stuck with me.

I did not need to be in the business of fixing broken men.

No, thanks.

Nope.

Can't do it.

So maybe he was right about it being a mistake. Even if it had felt so damn good.

"Just sleep." He flipped off the lamp near the bed, and the cabin went dark. I heard the couch creak, and soft grunts from him when he curled his large body up onto the cushions.

All I could do was turn over and sigh. Everything that had happened that day—getting lost, getting hurt, *him*—just kept repeating in my mind.

But I kept coming back to one thing:

Something or someone fucked him up. Badly.

<u>Chapter Six</u>

James

My dreams betrayed me that night.

In my restless slumber, I did *everything* with Keeley I had *wanted* to.

Our bodies were a tangle of heat and sex. I fucked her on the bed, and her body wrapped around mine as tight as any glove. Each time I sank into her, that beautiful mouth moaned and whimpered like she had when I'd only used my fingers to get her off.

It felt... different than it usually did. With other women, sex was fun—an experiment, a way to pass the time and blow off steam.

With Keeley, it was intimate. It was close. When I looked into her eyes, or felt her hands on me, my heart thundered loudly in my chest, and it was intense. Unstoppable.

When the morning sun hit me, I was pissed off that those feelings and images had all been experienced in a damn dream. I was stiff, in more ways than one. I had curled up on my way-too-small couch and fallen asleep there.

Well, I'd *eventually* fallen asleep, after a few angry hours, going over all the ways I'd fucked up my life to this point.

That was something I found myself doing way too much lately.

I sniffed, and then took a deeper breath. There was a smell in the air I didn't recognize at first. Warm and sweet. Damn, it smelled *good*. Like *home*.

I thought it might be pancakes. Where the fuck did *those* come from?

Keeley. *Right.*

She was awake already. After I rubbed my eyes, I unfolded myself from the couch and saw her on my bed, sitting against the headboard, cradling a book against her knees.

She didn't say a word. She didn't even look my way. And I couldn't fucking blame her.

I stumbled to the kitchen as I did every

morning, to make coffee and wake up. Except when I got there, the carafe was already hot and half-full. There was a stack of pancakes in the cast iron pan, and warm maple syrup in a small pot.

Clearly, I'd slept through *a lot.*

"You cooked in here?" I didn't mean for it to sound so *accusing.* But I fucked *that* up, too.

"Yes." It was a short, hard answer. It wasn't hard to tell she was in no mood to talk with me.

For whatever stupid reason, I kept trying. "You're up early," I observed, pulling a mug out of the cabinet.

It took her a minute to decide whether to respond. "I always get up early." She still didn't look up from her book. "Part of my job."

Right. I sipped the coffee. It was better than any I ever made, that was for damn sure.

I wanted to talk to her, but I didn't even know what to say. I told her the truth the night before. She deserved better than any of this. She didn't deserve to get hurt by that rockslide, or by me. It was just crazy chance that threw her my way.

All I had to do was not fuck up too much more until I could get her home. Hopefully I could make that work, at least.

She sat in the bed, reading intently, and the morning light fell on her golden skin. I should have looked away, but I drank in the sight of her on top of my old quilt.

Whoever let her go—and *someone* had, I knew that much—was a complete idiot. *Just like me.*

I watched her flip the pages of the book, and something fell out. She held it up to the light, and I could see what it was.

It was a postcard, an image of Winged Victory, from the Louvre. The statue's marble wings were spread wide, half in shadow.

The card was from my sister.

Something surged inside of me when I saw it. Anger or pain, whatever it was—it was fiery and caustic, and I couldn't hold it in.

"Don't read that!" I set my coffee mug down on the counter, hard, and stalked toward her.

She finally looked up. Her eyes were narrowed, her mouth a tight line. She took the postcard between her fingers and threw it at me. It fluttered in the air and landed on the floor between us.

Part of me wanted to reach for it. Part of me wanted to reach for *her.* But I didn't do anything. I just stood there, waiting, and I couldn't even look at her.

She closed the book and stood up. "I'm going to use your shower."

Her cut leg took her weight, but she still limped toward the bathroom door.

I didn't think she wanted my help. "Mind your bandage," I said. "Try not to get it wet."

She slammed the door behind her without a word. I heard the pipes creak when she turned on the water.

I bent to pick up the postcard and flipped it over. Olivia's handwriting was scrawled along the back in faded ink.

Jamie—

The patisseries here are like nothing you've ever seen. School is everything I hoped for so far. I'm finally doing it! LIVing the dream (see what I did there?). I visited the Louvre, but it would have been so much better with you. I'm pretty sure you could have told me about the techniques of every single artist. Keep saving up and hopefully we can get you here for a visit. Your dream could happen here, too.

I miss you.

Liv

My ribs felt like they were clenching around my heart. *I miss you, too, Liv. I miss what we used to be.*

She'd been my best friend when we were kids. She'd actually been my *only* friend. I never seemed to fit in. Pale and skinny and short, I cared more about art than sports or popularity. Art was my refuge from my parents, who didn't pay much attention to *either of us.* School was where the only kids who paid attention to me were bullies.

Liv had been my protector then. She was older and not as much of a misfit as I was. Somehow, she'd figured it all out in a way I never could, and she'd watched my back. But only for my freshman year—she was three years older, and when she graduated, I was alone.

When she left high school, everything got worse. It got physical.

Hard shoves.

Pushes into lockers.

When I could get my parents to listen to me, they brushed it off. *Toughen up. Ignore it.* They hadn't had a single protective instinct to protect their child. Never had.

Once the mean kids in school saw that I'd just take it, they wanted to know how far they could go.

One day, I walked back home, blood in my nose and eyes from a bullying session. Olivia was there, home from her job at the bakery. The look on her face when she saw me... I'd never forget *that look.*

It was the *same look* she'd given me the last time she had ever spoken to me.

She was horrified.

My sister had taken me to the emergency room, and waited with me while they checked me out, and cleaned my wounds. I was mostly all right—some bruised ribs, a black eye, nothing that wouldn't heal. At least, I was *physically* all right. Mentally? I was just checked out. I had all these fears, all this anger, and no clue what to do with it.

And I had felt the rage seething from Liv, too. It didn't stop when she took me home, and when she told our parents what had happened.

As usual, my mother and father didn't know how to respond. I didn't know whether they tried to understand, or they didn't. All I knew is they didn't lift a finger to make the bullying stop.

Liv told me to just wait. "*None* of these people matter, Jamie. One day you'll be on your own, a famous artist, and you'll be happy."

"What about you?" I'd mumbled through my

swollen, cut lips. "Why aren't you on your own?"

She'd sighed. "Can't afford it yet. And no, I'm not happy yet, either. But I'm working on it." She smiled, but her eyes were so sad. I could tell she was trying to put on a happy face for me. "You've got your dream, and I've got mine. You're going to be a great artist."

I tried to smile back, but it hurt too much. "And you're going to make the best cakes anyone ever tasted."

She'd ruffled my curly hair. "I'll always save you a slice, Jamie."

She *had* made me feel better. In truth, Liv had been the only thing that had gotten me through those horrible years.

And my situation improved...slowly.

I got tall, and wide. I worked summer jobs after school in a warehouse, and it built real muscle. I experienced one of those growth spurts that seemed to make everyone reevaluate me. Especially the people who used to beat me up. Once I towered over them, no one touched me. During those years, I'd learned one very sad fact—bullies only prey on those physically weaker than themselves.

I'd grown and filled out until I wasn't a skinny

little weirdo anymore.

I was a big, scary weirdo.

Liv had finally applied to a pastry school in Paris, took out a big loan, and left to pursue her dreams. I was so proud of her. I'd really wanted to visit her, but I could never save enough. I had to settle for postcards.

I ran a finger along the worn paper in my hand. *Like this one.*

One day you'll be on your own, a famous artist, and you'll be happy. I'd believed her. Until the day that I'd done something to scare her away from me entirely.

After what happened... maybe we could *never* go back to being what we used to be. Maybe I'd never be happy without Liv in my life. Probably... not.

The shower creaked again, and the water stopped.

I heaved a huge sigh.

Now there was *this.* Keeley was angry with me, for damn good reasons. I felt helpless, and angry, too.

That was the weird thing. I shouldn't feel *anything* at all. *Because I never did.*

Maybe I felt responsible for Keeley because I'd saved her. I let out a grunt of disgust. I was pretty sure *'responsible for anyone but me'* was what I came out here to *avoid.*

I needed to get back to what I *understood.*

Being alone.

Being responsible for nobody except myself.

And creating my art completely unencumbered.

I moved toward the kitchen. The pancakes were still warm, and so was the maple syrup. I piled them onto the plate, poured the syrup, refilled my coffee and grabbed a fork. I took all of it outside and headed to my workspace.

I needed to stop thinking.

Chapter Seven

Keeley

James had been outside all morning. I could hear the chipping and sanding from his woodcarving, and the occasional grunt of frustration. Other than that, he was silent. He left me alone.

And I was fine with that. I knew it sounded incredibly weird, especially considering the circumstances, but...

I was actually enjoying myself.

After I showered and dug out whatever extra clothes I was smart enough to put in my backpack yesterday, I made the bed and moved to the couch.

Yes, *that* couch, where he'd... Well, I wasn't thinking about *that* right now.

I was drinking decent enough coffee. I was

spread out on the couch with the window open beside me, a fresh breeze blowing in. I had put on one of my sheet masks—maybe I *was* smart to bring those, after all. I was reading whatever I could find, and most of it was pretty good.

I had nothing to do and nowhere to go. No responsibilities, no deadlines, no phone calls.

It was crazy. It only took being lost in the woods with no way out for me to finally relax.

It made me think that if I'd just stayed at that beautiful cabin, I might have started to enjoy it. To relax there and get used to being alone, and the quiet.

But maybe it had taken something *extreme* to get me to this point. I couldn't begin to guess.

All I knew was... I felt okay. My leg was sore, I was wearing a mixed-up mess of clothes, and I was stuck here. For now, I was good with that. I guess I *had* to be.

Ignoring him this morning, being angry with him, was all still there in my mind, too. I was more confused than angry now. Mostly, I was confused by *myself*. I didn't want to be here, but I liked it. I didn't want *him*, but the thought of his hands on me made me feel hot all over.

I had to stop thinking about how it had felt

when he touched me last night!

I went to the bathroom to take off the mask, and while I massaged the leftover serum into my skin, I grimaced at myself in the mirror.

Get it together, Keeley. This is not *how you meet new boyfriends. And this guy... is not right. In any way. You cannot fix a man who's broken. You know that. Don't even try it.*

But part of me said he wasn't all that broken, that he was driven by some kind of past pain. It wasn't the part of me that was turned on by him, either. It was something deeper that told me that James was wounded, but he wasn't completely broken.

I went back to the couch before I got into another argument with myself.

I tried to focus on the book in front of me, something dense and emotional and Russian, but the words blurred on the page.

If only there wasn't this cloud hanging over everything. James, everything that happened last night, the things I didn't want to think about kept creeping back into my mind.

Maybe *my ex* was the right type of guy for me after all. He was nice. He didn't confuse me. He let me know what he wanted, and when, and waited for me to reply with confirmation.

It was... scheduled. It was kind of like work. It didn't catch me off guard. It wasn't frantic, and volatile. It didn't feel like being *burned.*

Which one was worse? Scheduled activities, or complete volatility? I had no idea.

But there was only one man I couldn't stop thinking about. And it was not my ex.

Whatever. I pulled my legs up on the couch and turned the page, desperate to get back to the state of calm I'd experienced earlier.

The door creaked open behind me. I didn't turn around. Even though I *wanted* to.

"Hey, uh... Keeley." James said it softly, and something flipped in my stomach when I heard my name come from his beautiful mouth.

"Yeah?"

"Come out here for a minute."

What the hell? I turned around to see if there was anything I could read from his expression.

This friendly, beckoning tone was new, and I had no idea what he wanted from me.

I *shouldn't* have turned around. *God, he was gorgeous.*

His hair was wavy and dark, pulled back from his face, and his cheeks and neck were flushed pink from exertion. He looked at me with a kind of embarrassed half-smile, like he expected me to tell him to fuck off.

But I couldn't do that.

He was so fucking masculine and compelling. I hated it. It threw me off-balance.

"Why?" My tone was suspicious.

"Just..." He shook his head and walked over to me. "You won't regret it." He held out his hand to me. It was dusty and etched with little pink scars from his carving.

You won't regret it. Somehow I doubted that. If I could get out of this weekend stuck with him without regrets, *that* would be a serious accomplishment.

But I took his hand anyway because I couldn't resist. Not when he was talking to me so sweetly, which was yet another facet of his personality I'd never seen before. His rough fingers wrapped around mine, and he gently pulled me up from the couch. I stood close enough to him to smell the wood he was carving, and the fresh outside air that stayed on his skin.

He placed his large hand on my back. It

was warm between my shoulder blades, and I instinctively leaned into it. He urged me toward the door, and we walked outside.

His purpose wasn't work related because he led me past his carving table, and down a worn path overgrown with weeds. We pushed aside the bushes, and then he halted in front of me. He looked at me intently, and whispered huskily, "Be quiet."

I nodded, but I had no clue what was going on.

He parted another bush, crouched low and motioned me to come forward. I crouched, too, and looked at him expectantly. I felt a twinge of pain from my injury, but I easily ignored it. I was too curious about what he wanted me to see.

Past him, there was a dusty bank leading down into a small blue pond. He pointed across the water.

On the other bank, there were two soft brown elk standing in the shallow water. Their necks were bent toward the water and they drank quietly. Water dripped from their soft snouts. If they noticed us at all, they didn't feel threatened by our presence.

It was such a peaceful image. Their slow, gentle movements made me feel calm. They made me think about my own life—how hectic it was, how I approached things with so much anxiety. I held on too tight; I tried to control everything. I had an app that counted how much water I drank for God's sake. I couldn't even do *that* naturally.

I guess that Yasmin had been right. It was possible for my soul to be still and quiet. I was listening to my thoughts *now*, and they were telling me how much I *didn't* like my life.

But even now, I was ignoring what was in front of me. I couldn't solve all my problems at the moment. However, I could enjoy the peace that watching the elk brought me.

I turned to say something to James. I expected that he was watching the elk, just like I was. Instead, he was watching *me*. When our eyes met, he stared at me for a moment, and I saw his jaw twitch. He quickly turned his eyes away, toward the pond.

It was the same look he'd given me when he'd bandaged my leg. That look that burned right through me.

I *still* wanted him more than I'd ever wanted any man in my life. That was another problem I didn't know how to solve, but I realized I didn't have to. Not right now.

"Thank you," I whispered to James.

He shrugged. "Since you're here," he said, his voice low, "it would be a shame if you missed it."

He was right. But it wasn't just the sight of something I'd never seen before that I was talking about, what I was thanking him for.

We watched the elk in silence. They drank deeply of the pond, and when they were finished, they slowly backed out of the water and walked into the woods, picking their way through the wild weeds.

Eventually, we started making our way back to the cabin. I tripped over a root in the path, and James set his hand against my back again to steady me.

"You all right?" he asked. He didn't just sound polite. He actually sounded concerned about me.

I swallowed hard. How long had it been since a guy had cared about my welfare?

"I'm totally fine." I stood up straight and pulled myself away from his hand, walking on ahead of him. I didn't know what I was encouraging, and I wanted to avoid those regrets I feared so much. I only hoped he would keep acting human. Even if I *wanted* more... maybe I *needed* more... it was a bad idea.

It seemed that I couldn't really be around James *without* wanting more.

He just came closer to me instead of backing off. "Do you, uh, need anything?"

I stopped and turned to face him. "No. I'm good. I don't need... anything." *Certainly not you. Not at all.*

What the hell? Now I was lying to myself.

Right now, I could feel how lonely I'd been, and I'd never realized it. Yeah, I was around people all the time, but they always wanted something from me, except for my friends. My ex and I had been more like acquaintances who didn't talk all that much. The passion—if there had ever actually been some—had been long gone.

Don't think about your strange connection with James. And for God's sake, don't think about the fact that one touch from him makes every cell in your body jump to attention.

That was hard to do when I could hear his quiet steps at a distance behind me, like I was one of those thirsty elks he didn't want to scare off.

Unfortunately, I wasn't an elk.

I couldn't pretend he wasn't there anymore.

Chapter Eight

James

I was almost getting used to her.

Sometimes, for a few moments, I would forget Keeley was even there. *Okay. Yeah.* I could always *feel* her presence, but it didn't bother me that somebody was invading my space anymore. I'd been outside most of the afternoon, and she'd been quiet.

Then, I would come in for water, or food, and I'd see her, her golden legs stretched out on the couch, and her slender fingers caressing the edge of a book. She would brush that beautiful, silky hair from her face occasionally. Watching her, I felt myself grow hungry, and desperate, my cock swelling to the point of discomfort.

It took all my willpower not to walk over to that

couch and finish what I'd started the night before.

As for her? She didn't seem to notice me. She kept to herself and didn't ask for anything.

She didn't have to. I knew what she wanted— to go home.

I'd tried to call the rangers a few times and checked on the emergency lines to see if there was any news about the rockslide.

Maybe they'd gotten out there early.

Maybe it wasn't as bad as it looked.

Every time, there was no news. *We're getting to it. Sit tight.* They had enough to deal with without me bugging them. But I had to make sure we knew the latest. The radio was right in front of her, and it was a small cabin. She heard all my calls. She knew I was at least trying to give her what she wanted.

She probably thought I was eager to hear something for my own sake, that I still wanted her far away from here. Like I had when I first brought her back to my cabin bleeding and unconscious.

That wasn't it. Like I said, I was getting used to having her around. I wanted to talk to her. I *wanted her.*

I didn't like it when she said she didn't *need*

anything. Maybe because I had the insane urge to give Keeley anything and everything just to see her sweet, genuine smile again. And I hated the distance that had been put between us because I'd either hurt her or pissed her off the night before. Hell, maybe I'd done both, and that was why she was so standoffish.

I'd been alone too damn long. Acting like a normal person was never my strong suit, even as a kid. Now? I was basically a caveman. I ate and slept and made art. It wasn't the kind of life most people would want or understand.

It definitely wasn't the kind of life anyone would want to *share.* I had nothing to offer.

I'd deliberately designed it that way.

I guessed that's why I brought her to see the elk. It was a kind of apology, something I had that she might like. Something she'd probably never seen. A way to make up for being such an asshole.

And it seemed like she had enjoyed it. Her eyes had softened, and she'd smiled wistfully as she watched the animals. That action had nearly melted my stone-cold heart.

I couldn't help watching her again as we arrived back at the cabin. She was so damn beautiful that it was hard for me to turn my eyes away from her.

For the first time in years, I actually had the urge to paint. I wanted a way to capture all her colors—honey gold, cocoa brown, and berry red, warm and sweet in the sun.

Maybe I *would* paint her when she left.

You're insane, man. Paint yourself a memento of a woman you hardly know? Yeah. Normal never *was* my thing.

***

Night fell quickly. Keeley had been here over twenty-four hours. Just one more day and, if it went like the rangers said, she'd be gone.

I wasn't sure why the thought of her leaving gnawed at me until I was ready to snarl with discomfort.

I asked if she wanted something other than sandwiches for dinner, if I could *find* anything else. She set down her book and pushed off the couch.

"Let me figure something out," she suggested.

I didn't want her to do that. She'd already made pancakes. I'd never even thanked her for that. And they'd been really fucking good.

She came into the kitchen and started opening cabinets and poking around in my fridge. I sidestepped her and leaned on the counter. "I, uh, don't have much here. I need to get into town for supplies."

"I'm sure you've got something." She bent over, searching through my nearly empty refrigerator, and I wasn't too proud to take a long look at her gorgeous ass.

I wanted to remember *that*, too. Although I doubted that I'd actually *paint it.*

She turned around holding a carton of eggs, and some bacon. "Is this bacon ridiculously old and gross, or is it okay?"

I huffed a short laugh. "It's okay."

"That's a start," she said, placing the items on the counter. "Thought I saw some spaghetti when I found the flour earlier..." She looked up into a tall cabinet and tried to stand on her toes to reach the highest shelf. She winced, and I felt like shit because she was in pain. Her leg still seemed to be sore.

"Here." I walked over to the cabinet, and stood close to her, my arm on her shoulder to hold her back. "Let me."

Her wide brown eyes traveled over my chest. It felt almost as good to have her look *me* over as it felt to look at her.

For a moment, I actually felt wanted, and it was a damn heady sensation.

I wanted to pull her close, to lean down and claim her mouth. I wanted to lift her up onto the counter and wrap her legs around me. To feel her, inside and out, and make her scream my name.

Mine! Keeley doesn't belong with anyone else but me.

My very next thought was:

Fuck. No.

I was having a hard time fighting my conflicting emotions, and my relentless need to claim this woman for my own.

I have no right to own this woman. To make her exclusively mine. But damned if I didn't want that just the same.

I reached up and found the pasta and brought it down to her.

She took it from my hand, and when both of hers wrapped around the box, her fingers brushed mine. There was a soft flush on her cheeks that was so damn adorable that I wanted to fuck her right there in the tiny kitchen. "Well," she said, with a crooked smile, "I think I can do something with this."

I'm sure you can.

Before I completely lost my shit, I backed away and left the kitchen to her.

It was hard enough not to watch her when she was doing *nothing*. When she was cooking, making something out of nothing, and doing it all with confidence and ease... it was kind of spellbinding.

I tried really hard not to look at her again, but I could smell some amazing aromas coming out of the kitchen as she cooked.

Soon enough, she handed me a plate with a crooked smile, an expression that I'd learned was happiness, mixed with a little bit of uncertainty.

That smile made my gut ache.

"Carbonara. Kind of, anyway," she murmured.

Even if it was only *kind of*, it looked and smelled incredible. Better than anything I could have come up with.

"Thanks. This is, uh... you didn't have to." I felt sheepish all of a sudden, like she could see everything in my thoughts.

That quizzical stare always disarmed me, so I looked away.

She snorted. "Oh, I did have to. I didn't really

want another sandwich. No offense."

"Believe me, none taken." Hell, I'd been eating almost nothing but cold sandwiches for years.

We sat at my table and ate quietly for a while. I was grateful for the quiet. It was kind of comfortable, having dinner here with her. Almost natural. I didn't know what to make of that, so I decided to just concentrate on my food.

The *kind-of-carbonara* was fucking delicious. That helped keep my mind off her while I ate.

I should learn to make something except sandwiches.

I'd always been hopeless at cooking. I was impressed with Keeley's skill, and I told her so.

"You could do it, too. It's pretty easy, really."

"Nah." I shook my head and looked away. "I think my sister got all of the culinary talent." Liv could make anything.

I stared at the dark window, out at the quiet night. I wondered if my sister was still baking these days... if that still made her happy.

"Your sister likes to cook?" From inside the fog of my thoughts, Keeley sounded far away.

Why did I even say that out loud? I didn't want to talk about Olivia. I didn't even want to *think* about her.

My mind was suddenly everywhere. Like I said, I'd been alone too long. Having someone else around, in my space, had me feeling like I wanted to communicate with another soul. Maybe I was temporarily insane because Keeley was here. I really didn't want to be close to anyone.

One minute I liked her being here; the next I couldn't stand it.

I thought maybe I wouldn't answer her, and just keep eating my food. But she looked at me expectantly, waiting for me to respond.

Like a normal person would do.

I swallowed. "I don't really want to talk about her."

Her brow furrowed, then she nodded, and turned back to her food. She didn't push me on it. I don't know what I expected, but my face was hot. With embarrassment? I didn't even know anymore. I turned back to the window.

What I really didn't like talking about was how I felt, *ever*.

"You know, I really kind of like it here," Keeley mused aloud.

Wait a minute... what?

Keeley's voice was bright and sunny, and she smiled at me. It seemed like she was trying to change the subject. Maybe I had made her uncomfortable. Probably wouldn't be the last time.

Or maybe she was doing it for me. Could she tell how much talking about Liv bothered me?

Shit, *that* was hard to believe. No one had cared how I felt in so long. A lot of times, even I didn't care much about myself.

"All things considered," she said, "I'm kind of having a nice time."

I cocked my head in disbelief. "Really?"

"I'm more surprised than you are." She pushed away her empty plate. "It's... quiet. I guess I can see why you live here. I guess that's what I'm saying."

"But you..." I scratched at my beard, at my too-long hair that itched at my collar. "You don't need to be out here. I'm sure you're wanted back home."

And if you're not, L.A. is worse than I thought.

She looked at me for a moment, her sweet mouth opened slightly. There was a flash of sadness in her eyes. "Do you *need* to be here?" I asked hesitantly, not sure why I had to know.

She swallowed. "I think so."

Her brow wrinkled, and her nose scrunched up. She shook her head. "I don't understand it, but I feel like I was *meant* to be here right now."

Something shifted in me. She was beautiful, and I wanted her—that was easy enough to process and ignore when it grew too intense. Beneath that, though, way deeper than my simple desire to fuck her, my mind was telling me something else. Maybe it was some kind of mysterious connection that drew my sorry ass to her.

I *wanted* to tell her everything. I *wanted* her to understand me.

And that scared the hell out of me.

"I fucked up, Keeley," I said, my voice breaking in my throat. "Really bad."

Keeley leaned on her fist and looked at me, her dark brown eyes clear and open, and giving. "You can tell me."

Even though it went against my better judgment, I did. I told her *everything.*

Chapter Nine

James

It had been the holidays, almost nine years ago, and I'd been home with my parents—and we were doing what we always did—ignoring each other.

Liv was home for the holidays, too. She'd been back from Paris for a couple of years, though I hadn't seen her much. I was busy finishing art school, trying to establish some kind of career, finally finding a place where I could do what I wanted. Be who I wanted to be.

We'd been happy to see each other that Christmas. Too bad I hadn't been so thrilled about her new *boyfriend.*

I grimaced. Even now, I could still remember how condescending he'd been to Olivia. And how fucking patronizing he'd been about *my art.* But

I'd managed to hold back on my instincts...in the beginning. After all, it was nothing a few whiskeys couldn't help me tune out.

Then, I'd noticed the bruises on Olivia's wrists, saw the way she covered and cowered at her boyfriend's constant criticism. It had been enough to send me into an ugly rage.

When I'd heard Olivia and her boyfriend fighting in her childhood bedroom, I'd finally lost my shit.

I hadn't cared if he threw barbs at me, but when he started on my sister, I'd been done ignoring the bastard.

I hadn't bothered to check myself. *At all.*

I'd stomped to the bedroom. All it had taken was the sight of the big man standing over Olivia, her hands swiping at her tear-stained face, and it was *on.* I'd slammed the asshole into the wall. I'd bashed his face, over and over. Broke his nose, and his jaw.

The son of a bitch had begged me to stop, but I hadn't. I couldn't. I was in a blind rage over what he'd done to the sister who had always been there for me when I was a child.

She'd protected me when I was a kid, so I had the driving urge to do the same for her as an adult.

Finally, my father had pulled me off him, and even *then*, I hadn't been ready to stop.

I could remember Olivia crying hysterically from her seat on the bed.

All I'd really wanted to do was comfort her, make sure she was okay, see if she needed anything.

However, the moment I'd sat down next to her, she'd backed away, choking out breathless sobs as she went.

Holy shit! I'd forever remember the look of horror on her face, the expression of *absolute disbelief.*

But the thing that lingered the clearest in my mind was her *fear*. Of *me*. She'd moved away from me like *I was* the monster.

I hadn't seen her *since that day.* Or my parents, either, since they seemed to be scared of the mindless rage I hadn't been able to control, too.

It was the one time they seemed to show any emotion at all.

I'd heard that Liv had eventually married the asshole. Obviously, I hadn't been invited to the wedding, but I was constantly haunted by images of her getting beaten up so badly that she ended up in the hospital. *Or worse.*

But what in the hell could I do about that since she refused to even let me near her?

I didn't understand it at all.

She was the one who had helped me when I was bullied. Who'd protected me. She'd seen what it had done to me, and *she'd* always stepped in without hesitation.

How could she let *herself* be hurt like that? *How could she love someone like that?*

Maybe I hadn't needed to thrash him as badly as I had, but I sure as hell had *never* regretted it. I would have hated myself more if I'd done nothing, or worse yet, tried to actually reason with a guy who had no reasoning ability because he was an abusive bastard.

In my mind, Olivia's boyfriend had gotten *exactly* what he deserved.

Still, I'd tormented myself, wondering if there hadn't been a small part of me that enjoyed kicking his ass. Had I wanted blood on my hands? Had I done it not to defend Olivia, but because I'd wanted to do it for myself?

Had I become just another bully?

Was I really a monster?

After that, I'd gone down a slippery slope into

a pretty dark place. People hadn't made sense to me anymore. After long hours in my studio, alone with my own scary thoughts, I'd had no idea who I even was anymore.

I felt out of place. Out of time. Like I didn't belong *anywhere*.

Truth was, sometimes *I was scared* of what was inside me, too.

Honestly, I *had* been out of control that night, and I hadn't liked the person I'd turned into. I couldn't reconcile the two—the justified rage, *and* the blinding one.

After that Christmas, I'd needed to get away. Being alone was easier. Living alone made sense. I couldn't hurt anyone else if there was nobody around me.

Once I'd bailed myself out of jail, and paid the price for what I'd done, I'd checked out of civilization for a planned one-year break that had turned into a very long period of solitude.

However, there was one thing that I couldn't get out of my mind. Something stuck with me and haunted me.

When Olivia had backed away from me, terrified, all I could think was that I couldn't understand *her* anymore.

How in the hell had we grown so far apart?

"What happened to your dream, Liv? What about being happy?" I'd asked her once she'd moved away from me that evening.

She'd stared back at me, and then gaped at her fiancé's blood on my fists. She looked at me like she felt the same as I did—that I didn't make any sense to *her*. That I wasn't her brother anymore. Like I was some kind of maniacal stranger.

Her voice was stern when she finally replied, "This is what I want now. You almost took that away from me. I won't let you. I hate you. Stay away from me."

Right then, I realized how much *she* had changed. How much we *both* had.

The one person who had always loved me unconditionally was gone.

I was suddenly alone, and completely destroyed.

Chapter Ten

Keeley

The story James told me was nothing like I expected.

When he'd finished, he stared down at the table between us, his arms folded tight. He wouldn't look at me. I suppose he thought I was judging him.

Honestly, I'd gotten over the stupid idea that he was a psycho killer. Having an anger problem... feeling betrayed by your family... wanting to protect the ones you love... None of those things make someone a psycho.

The way he talked about it; he was definitely still in pain. Guilt and regret followed him around like a dark cloud. That's how it seemed to me.

The regret was the potent thing. That was what

made him so afraid of *everything*. Even himself.

He's so afraid of himself. Of what he might do. He doesn't realize that everyone has a breaking point where they lose control.

In his case, I thought his actions were more than justified.

I wasn't afraid of *him*. Whatever he said, he didn't seem *dangerous* to me.

Never once had James lost his temper and gone off on me, even though I knew my presence was something he definitely *didn't* want.

All I could judge was what I saw in front of me. Sure, I didn't *know* him. I only met him the day before—in the weirdest circumstances imaginable. However, I wasn't about to judge a man for losing it trying to protect his sister from injury...or death.

He can't keep blaming himself and seeing himself as some kind of monster.

He'd saved my life. I thought I could do something for him in return.

"Can I tell you something?" I asked.

He didn't say anything. He didn't look up. So I went on.

"I have this friend. She had a boyfriend who

would get rough with her. He would grab her too hard, raise his voice too much. I don't know what else he did at home," I said. "I guess I was afraid to know."

That person was my friend, Yasmin. The one who convinced me to go on this wild trip. My fingers tapped nervously against the table as I remembered the things I used to hear from her. I remembered how powerless and angry I felt.

"He was such an asshole. But she wouldn't break up with him."

James finally looked up. He was listening to me. I hoped he could really *hear* what I was saying. I hoped it made sense to him.

"We were out at a bar one night, and he started acting like that. She just sat there and took it." I shook my head, my jaw tight as I continued to tell the story.

"It made me crazy. But I wasn't mad at *her*," I stressed to him. "I wanted to help her, but... it doesn't make sense to you if you're not the one it happens to. That's what she told me later. You think you'd never let it happen to you, but you don't know. How could you?"

His dark blue eyes looked at me with concern. Still, he was quiet, and listened.

"Anyway, I was beyond pissed that night. He wouldn't leave her alone. And maybe I'd been drinking a little too much, but..." I winced, remembering everything that happened.

"I smashed a bottle over his head."

His eyebrows raised. "Damn," he rasped.

I sighed. "Yeah. Then he tried to beat *me* up. We both got arrested."

He placed his hands on the table, his body appearing tense. "Were you all right?"

"Oh," I said, waving my hand. "I was fine. I wish I could say that was the last straw for Yasmin. But it took a little while for it to sink in. You know?"

"Yeah." He nodded softly and his brow furrowed.

"Your sister might've just needed time, James? And I know it doesn't change anything, but your heart was in the right place," I said. I leaned my elbows on the table. "I'm sure it still is."

"How can you be sure of that?" His voice was barely a hoarse whisper.

To me, it seemed so simple. "You *saved* me. And I think you wanted to save *her*, too."

He looked up at me, the disbelief clear on his face. "I'm the asshole who sent you off to get hurt in the first place, Keeley. You were in trouble. Anyone would have helped you."

I scoffed. "No, they wouldn't. But *you* did. You're *not* a bad person. Even if you've thought that for a long time, that doesn't make it true."

I knew I was taking a risk, trying to convince him of something about himself, when I barely knew him. The thing was, I'd kind of been where *he'd* been. Yasmin wasn't my sister, and my situation wasn't as extreme, but I knew how he felt—like you were pointing to something obvious that no one else seems to see. Like no one made sense.

His gaze veered away, and he stared out at the dark night.

I stood up slowly and picked up the plates. "I'm gonna leave you alone for a little while. Let me know if you want to talk about it more."

He sat at the table for a few minutes while I began washing the dishes and cleaning up, and then he stood. He went to the bookshelf, pushed aside a few dusty novels, and took down a stack of postcards. I watched him from time to time while I washed. He sat on the couch and read them, one by one, and finally heaved a masculine sigh.

There wasn't much to clean. When I finished, he was still there, thinking, the pile of postcards in his lap. I walked over, and he looked up, his eyes hazy.

"I was afraid of myself, Keeley. I lost complete control. I had absolutely no rational thought when I was beating the guy senseless. All I could think about was him hurting Liv. I didn't know when to stop. I had to wonder if there was something inherently evil inside me. Some part of me that I didn't know. If I actually liked hurting people."

My heart clenched. "You're not that man, James," I said quietly. "You aren't evil. You had a blind rage for a reason. Maybe I don't know you well, but you aren't going to hurt anybody else."

He looked at me like he wanted to believe me. "How do you know?"

I shrugged. "Instinct. I'm not afraid of you."

"You know," he began, his voice husky, "my sister and I were all we had. And then I lost her. I don't know if I can get back to that place, but... if you think I've changed... maybe she has, too."

My chest was pounding hard as I looked at him. "It's a risk," I advised. "She may not have changed, and you'll need to move on."

He shrugged. "Then I guess I'll have to close

that relationship. But at least I'll know. Better than wondering, I guess."

Wow. That was a shift. And it was a welcome one. "Maybe you should look for her. Maybe she's been looking for you. You're not all that easy to find." I tried to sound gentle, but I thought it was something he needed to hear. He'd isolated himself to the point where *nobody* could find him.

He nodded, and slowly collected the postcards back into a messy stack, placing them back on the shelf. Then he turned to me. "Do something for me. Would you?"

His neck was flushed, and his lips were parted. He stared at me, and *that look* was back—it smoldered and blazed right through me. I didn't know what he wanted, but I found myself hoping for a few things. I saw his nostrils flare as he waited for my answer.

"Depends on what," I said. My voice shook.

His mouth curled up in a wry half-smile. "Cut my hair."

Really? I had to choke back a surprised laugh. His request definitely wasn't what I'd expected. I must have looked at him like he was crazy, because he laughed and shook his head.

"It's getting annoying," he explained. "I just

want it all cut off so I can work without it hanging in my eyes. And it's the one thing I have trouble doing for myself."

"Oh, just that one thing?" The sarcasm came out before I could stop it.

He snorted. "Okay, that's fair. Still, though." That half-smile was still there, and it was irresistible. "Could you do it?"

I walked up to him and stood close—close enough to grab onto his flannel collar and pull him down for a full, wet kiss... if I wanted to. Something told me he wouldn't really mind that. He looked down at me, looking genuinely amused for the first time.

"Are you sure? Your hair looks really good long."

His eyes searched my face. "I'm sure," he said, his voice low.

I nodded. "Then get the stuff to do it."

Despite the heat in my cheeks and the butterflies in my stomach, I felt a twinge of pain in my leg, so I sat down on the edge of the mattress while he dug the things out of his bathroom cabinet. When he brought the scissors, a comb, and a towel to me, I knew James was deadly serious about losing his hair.

He stood back and unbuttoned the flannel. He looked at me the whole time. Watching him reveal that ripped, masculine body was intense, and my mouth went dry just watching him strip. Underneath, he wore a grey T-shirt, and he peeled that off, too.

Oh. My. God.

Shirtless, he was magnificent. The thick muscles in his arms and stomach tensed. My pulse throbbed in my neck...and lower.

I realized he wasn't teasing me, even though it felt like he was. James didn't have a clue how sexy he was at all. Unfortunately, for me, that made him even more attractive.

He walked up to me, and then he sat on the floor between my legs, his back against the bed. He wrapped the towel around his shoulders.

"Here?" I asked.

"Yeah. Here's good. You need to be somewhere that doesn't make your leg hurt."

There it was again, that concerned, rough voice that made my heart melt. James had trained himself not to give a fuck about anything except his art, but it had never completely worked because he *did* care. His heart had never changed. He'd just buried his emotions incredibly well.

And here goes nothing. I didn't think I'd ever cut anyone's hair before, except my own, and those were just trims and bangs. This was different. I figured cutting it all off couldn't be *that* hard. After all, he didn't exactly seem to care how it came off as long as it was out of his face.

I can do that.

I had a feeling that James wanted more than just a convenient haircut. Somehow, I felt like the action was symbolic. A small but important gesture that said he was getting ready to join civilization again someday.

I tried to keep my hands steady. For some reason, doing this simple task for him seemed more intimate than rolling around in bed satisfying our bodies.

My knees touched his shoulders when I leaned forward. I tentatively brushed through his hair with my fingers, the dark curls separating around them, and I felt what sounded like a low growl of satisfaction hum quietly through his body. I didn't even think he *meant* to make a sound. But he was obviously enjoying my touch.

It struck me that even if he'd been with other women, maybe no one had touched him like this in a long time. No one had simply caressed his hair or placed a hand on his arm softly. Gestures of affection and comfort rather than carnal and sexual actions.

Had anyone ever cared enough about James to just... touch him? For no reason other than affection?   His sister obviously had, but it had been a long time.

It was only then I thought about how lonely he must have been. He'd been out here in the woods alone for eight years.

Even though he was truly alone here, and I was in a crowded city, with friends and coworkers, surrounded by people—I was lonely, too.

I'd wanted some elusive...*something.*   Or maybe I'd needed...*someone.*

Shaking off those thoughts, I worked quickly. I cut off the long strands, and they fell onto the towel, and down to the floor.   Part of me was truly sad to see them go, but... there was something so intimate about this.   I felt the heat of his scalp against my fingers, his body against my legs, and his hands on the floor near my bare feet.

When his hair was short enough, I began to trim. In a few minutes, his long curls were gone. All that was left was short dark waves.

I brushed the stray hairs from his neck, and he removed the towel.

He turned to face me. "How does it look?"

Fucking... amazing.

He had been beautiful before, and that hadn't changed. But the deep sapphire of his eyes, and his flushed tanned skin were so clear without all that hair.

"Do you want to look in a mirror?" I managed to say.

He looked into my eyes and shook his head. "I trust you. If you like it, that's all that matters."

It kind of amazed me that a guy as smoking hot as James had no real vanity about his looks.

I couldn't stop myself from reaching out and stroking the short, soft hair. I scratched his scalp. His eyes drifted shut when I touched him. He took my hand in his and kissed it softly.

He was a guy of few words most of the time, so I knew it was his way of thanking me.

My breath caught in my throat. I wanted him, and he wanted me, that much was clear, but... I was caught off guard by how gentle he was. By how his dark blue eyes looked up at me, questioning.

He leaned forward and stroked my legs. His rough hands felt so good against my skin. I shivered at his touch and bit my lip.

He came closer, and his lips met my leg, grazing my knee, kissing just inside my thigh. The coarse hair of his beard brushed my skin, and it felt *so good.*

"I've wanted to do this, Keeley," he whispered against my skin in a low, sexy tone. "When I first had you here, I—" a soft kiss upon my thigh, a short groan— "I wanted to kiss you. I wanted to taste your skin."

My legs opened wider. It felt like an instinct. His hands found the outside of my thighs, and he gripped them in his large hands.

"Do you want this?" he asked in a hoarse voice. "Tell me you want this."

My breath quickened when his hands moved up toward my hips, and his fingers dug into the waistband of my shorts.

Do I?

Chapter Eleven

James

If she said no, I don't know what I would have done.

But she didn't.

Instead, she pulled closer to me, her thighs surrounding my head. It wasn't a bad place to be. She ran her soft hands over my shoulders, and I savored the touch.

"You know I do." Throaty and low, her voice was so fucking sexy that I looked up at her. Keeley's dark brown eyes glittered in the dim light.

I had said I wanted her, but that was a lie. *I fucking needed her.*

I had to find a way to stake my claim or I was going to lose it.

I wanted to own this woman, body and soul, which was probably a little bit creepy, but I couldn't help the desperate pain in my gut to possess her. Completely.

Keeley had heard what I had done, and she hadn't run away. There hadn't been even a flash of censure or distaste on her face. She listened, and told me she understood, that she'd been through something similar.

And...she fucking trusted me.

For the first time in a long while, I felt human. I felt like a *man* again instead of just an artist. *She* made me feel that way. Keeley made me hunger for something...more.

My fingers drifted along her waist, and I shuddered. Touching her was like tasting a decadent dessert—the more I had, the more I wanted.

I wanted to thank her for *seeing me*, but words seemed foolish. But this, the way I needed her—it wasn't a *thank you*. It was a *release*. It was a *statement*. I would show her *everything* I felt, even if I couldn't *say it*. I could find the shape of how I felt in her body, and in her pleasure.

Standing on my knees, I stretched up to kiss her. Her warm lips met mine, and she pulled and sucked at me like she was as famished as I was, like she needed to taste me, just like I needed to devour her.

My fingers found the button on her shorts and yanked it open. I knew I couldn't be gentle with her, and that she didn't want it right now. The desire was too fierce, too intense. I felt her trembling against me as I pulled down the zipper. I gripped the waistband of her shorts and her panties and pulled.

She broke the kiss and raised her hips. I eased the clothes down, careful of her bandage, and over her feet. I tossed them behind me, my eyes on her golden legs, and the soft, dark shadow between them.

Fuck. I licked my lips, and then looked into her eyes. They were heavy-lidded, drunk only with lust and wanting. She opened her legs further to me without me having to ask.

I bent down and kissed up her thigh, licking her smooth skin. Her scent was sweet and musky, and it pulled me closer.

My tongue found her sweet pussy, and I drank it in. *Like honey,* I had told her, and I had guessed right. *Fuck,* it was too good. My head was spinning, and her little whines and moans made the blood rush to my cock, making it impossibly harder.

Don't care about my cock right now. Need to make her come.

My breath sawed in and out of my lungs as I kept licking at her, squeezing her soft thighs in my hands. Feeling her folds against my flicking tongue.

Her breath was quick, coming in short, sharp gasps. I looked up at her, and saw her head thrown back, the sweat on her neck glistening in the dim light of the lamp.

Her fingers clawed at my shoulders, and found their way up my neck, to my scalp. Even her scratches felt like a sweet relief.

I leaned in further and pressed my tongue inside her. She let out a filthy groan. *"James,"* she called out, her voice full of dirty lust.

Oh, fuck me. There was something unbearably hot about the way my name sounded coming from her, between her moans of pleasure. I pulled away. "Say it again," I ordered, my voice harsh and deep, shaking with want. "Say my name."

She gasped and grunted when my tongue entered her again. "James! Oh, God, James!"

At that moment, I knew I was fucking lost.

It took everything I had not to pull my aching

cock out then... but I was concentrating on her. I wanted her to *feel* this, feel *me*. I wanted to satisfy her like no other even could, now, or in the future. The only guy I ever wanted her to think about when she was in this kind of lustful state was...me.

I circled her clit slowly. She bucked against my mouth and I held her steady, pushing her thighs down to the bed to open her wider. Then I sucked at it, pulling and nipping. Her moans broke in her throat, and I felt her legs tense and twitch.

Somehow, I jerked myself away, my breath hard and hot, and I knew she could feel it on her hot, wet pussy. "Keeley..." I lapped at her, wanting her taste again. "Come for me," I demanded. I had to watch her. I had to see it.

I fucking craved being the guy who made her come apart.

She fell back against the bed with a tormented moan, and pulled at my head, bringing me closer to her. *Demanding* I come closer.

I fucking loved it because she coveted my touch. Needed it. Wanted it so bad that it was making her crazy.

I sucked her swollen clit into my mouth again, rolling it against my tongue. Then she broke, her body arching under my hands. She cried out desperately, and her fists gripped the bedsheets.

I kept on and on, my tongue swirling madly against her to break her further. I wanted her to remember this for the rest of her life. I wanted her to think of me for months, for years, like I would think of her.

I wanted her to imagine that if she never would have left me, I would eat her sweet pussy every night until she screamed, just like this.

So many wild thoughts, half-formed, ran through my mind while she moaned and thrust herself against my mouth.

They were things I didn't think I wanted until they came to me.

Her body and breath slowed, and her moans quieted. She pushed my head away gently, like she couldn't take anymore. I sat back on my heels, my heart thundering against the wall of my chest.

I knew I *would* be thinking of her after she left. But did I really want her to think of me the same way?

Hell, yes, I did.

Did I honestly want her to never leave me? Had that thought come from somewhere deep within me, a desire that I wasn't even conscious of until now?

I didn't know what to think. My mind was a fog of lust and need. There was a beautiful, half-naked woman on my bed, and I had made her scream with desire and tasted all her pleasure. She was peeling off her shirt, and then her bra, and it was hard to think of anything but my heavy, hard cock as I became mesmerized while I watched her get completely naked.

So beautiful, and so fucking...mine.

My every instinct was hammering at me to make sure she belonged only to me. If that made me a greedy bastard...so be it.

I climbed onto the bed beside her, and she pulled me close. I kissed her, licked at her throat, and she gave a shaky sigh. Her arms wrapped around me, and I felt the heat of her body against mine, and her cool, plump lips kissing my fevered skin.

My body was throbbing with need.

But something in my mind held me back.

I trust you.

I remembered saying that to her before. I had said it about the haircut, but that's not what I had meant. Not really. It hadn't been said for simply hacking off my hair.

I had trusted her with my *story*, with the most painful, tormenting part of my life. I trusted what she said to me about her own experience.

And now, my mind was telling me I wanted even more from her—that I wanted her in my life, in one way or another. I wanted her to need me the way I fucking needed her.

That thought terrified the hell out of me.

I was the guy who just wanted to be alone.

But she was touching me, and the last damn thing I wanted was to be alone again. Her hands were massaging my chest and stomach. She inched farther down and found my hard cock through my pants. She squeezed and gripped me, and I couldn't help but let out a low groan. She eased me out of my jeans and held me in both her hands.

Fuck. It suddenly didn't matter how terrified I was. I didn't want her to stop.

She stroked me, slowly, her body moving against mine in time with her hands. Her soft, small hands on my cock, and her gentle pressure— it was maddening. I grunted and thrust into her hands. "Faster," I growled.

She did what I said. Her pace quickened,

and the pressure built in me, hot and urgent. She leaned into the crook of my neck, and her quickening breaths were sultry on my skin.

Then she licked my neck, and her teeth sharply grazed the skin. It was too damn much. My body shook, my thighs twitched. I let out a sharp groan. I came suddenly, and spilled heavily onto her hands, and on my stomach. It seemed to go on so long, and she kept stroking me, like she wanted me to find the end of my pleasure, to feel it fully.

I finally placed a hand on her arm to signal her to stop. I turned my head to look at her.

She lay there, head on my pillow, her dark eyes hazy, with a soft, crooked smile on her face.

I couldn't help myself. I took her face in my hands and kissed her. My hands wound into her silky hair, and I felt her sighing.

Jesus! Sexual gratification had never been like *this* before. Not when I was younger, and not in the years since I had lived here in the woods. Getting off was always a quick thing, a physical thing—in someone's tiny apartment, or a hotel room I couldn't wait to get out of.

It was never here, in my bed. There was never passion, or intimacy. No connection.

This... this was different. I felt something.

Whether it was fear, or something sweeter, or a strange combination of both... I felt it strongly.

It was something like what I felt when I was carving. There's an intensity there, and a purpose.

But this was better, because I could share it with someone else. With *her*.

I grimaced because I'd spilled myself like a damn teenager, without the chance to even get inside her body.

Luckily, she didn't even seem like she cared.

I grinned when I looked at her and saw that she was already in a deep sleep with a sweet smile on her face.

Chapter Twelve

Keeley

The bed was warm when I woke up. Sunlight streamed in through the half-curtained window. There was a hand resting on my naked hip.

James.

I didn't remember falling asleep next to him. Not that I didn't remember the night before at all. *Oh, hell yes, I did.* It had been everything I didn't know I wanted from him.

Intimate.

Intense.

Lusty and carnal.

Completely mind-blowing.

He was still asleep next to me, breathing deeply,

his head crooked on the pillow. The dark beard framed his lips so enticingly that I wanted to kiss him. Now I knew just how skilled those tempting lips of his really were.

I looked out the sunny window and thought about the last two days. He had been a jerk to me, and then he went above and beyond. He was weird, and then he was kind. He had spilled his guts out to me and told me things that clearly still hurt to think about.

Then, he had been sweet, and sexy, and... I squeezed my thighs together remembering last night.

It felt like we'd hardly begun to find out how we fit together. There was so much more I wanted to do with him, know about him...

Of course, he *would* have to wake up first.

There was a cool breeze that snuck in through the drafty window, and it hit my bare shoulders. There were birds singing outside, and I could hear the breeze pick up and grow stronger.

It was so beautiful here. So peaceful. Problem was, I didn't know if my contentment actually came from the place I was in, or the man lying next to me in bed.

I hadn't slept this hard in a *long* time. I couldn't

even remember my eyes closing the night before.

I smiled. If someone had told me a week ago I would end up lost and hurt in the woods, get stuck with a mountain man in a dingy cabin, and *liked it,* I would have told that person they were fucking crazy.

Something had changed since I got here. I suppose both of us, James and I, had changed a little. Both of us had been forced out of our comfort zones—even though it wasn't all that *comfortable.*

There was more to it than that, though. I'd had to trust him when he brought me out here after the rockslide.

Now, he seemed to trust *me,* too.

That meant something.

He stirred next to me, and his hand on my hip pulled me closer to him. He leaned in to kiss me, softly, nipping at my bottom lip.

I had definitely had worse wake-up calls.

"Good morning," he said in a sleepy, sexy baritone, nuzzling my ear. "Awake early again?"

I couldn't help but smile. "Usually I'm up way before sunrise." I stroked his cheek, and his eyes drifted shut at my touch. "We can't all be eccentric loners who make our own schedules, can we?"

He let out a soft chuckle and stroked my back. "Nope. Some of us are just lucky. You fell asleep on me last night."

"Looks like I did. Sorry."

He grunted a quiet response and stroked my hair. "It's okay. It gave me some time to think. You snore a little."

I looked up at him and pursed my lips. "I do not."

"If you say so," he said, a wry half-smile on his face.

I draped my arms around his neck and leaned against him. His rough hands stroked my skin, and I entwined my legs with his. Waking up with him like this felt so good that it was a little scary.

Because I knew it wouldn't last.

I was going to go home, to my empty apartment with the boho furnishings and the plants I didn't know how to take care of. Home to my job that stressed me out and took over my life.

If I wanted to enjoy this without thinking about the future for a few more hours, who would blame me?

"You know," he said, "I, uh, was thinking about what you said. About my sister."

"Oh?"

He nodded. "I *am* going to see if I can find her." He looked up at the ceiling and released a heavy breath. "Maybe she won't want to talk to me but... I'm going to try."

"That's great." He was taking the first steps. Maybe he just needed someone to understand how he felt. He'd told me his story like he was desperate for someone to hear him.

And there I was, ready to listen.

I had thought about his issues the first night—I don't go around fixing broken people or solving their problems for them. That never worked. I'd learned my lesson with Yasmin. These things take time. People need to fix themselves for it to stick.

However, there was nothing wrong with being there to listen.

"Another thing I was thinking about..." His hands drifted down my back and kept going. He caressed my ass and squeezed. I pushed my hips toward him and bit my lip.

"What is that?" I asked breathlessly.

I couldn't help how my body responded to him.

If I were a guy, it would be *really* damned obvious.

Clearly, his body was on the same page. His hard cock was pressed gently against my thigh.

He looked into my eyes. His own were clear, deep blue in the morning light. "Do you think you'll ever come back to Colorado?"

That was *not* the question I expected.

He brought a hand up to my cheek, and his fingers brushed against my jaw. "It's just... first the rockslide, then you had to deal with *me*." That half-smile was back. "Probably not the vacation you expected."

I laughed. "Not exactly."

We were quiet for a moment, just looking at each other. I didn't know how to answer his question. It wasn't an invitation, exactly.

Two days ago we wanted nothing to do with each other. I wanted out of here as much as he wanted me gone. Had things really changed that much in such a short time? Or were we just blinded by being close to each other, by the sweet simple pleasure of being naked in bed with someone you desired so badly?

Did he mean he *wanted* me to come back? Or was he just checking to make sure I still hated it?

Because I didn't hate it. *Not at all.*

I didn't have a clear answer for him. Not yet. At least, not until I knew *exactly* what he was asking.

His eyes searched mine, and there was a brief flash of worry in them. Then he smiled and kissed my forehead. "I'll be back in a few minutes."

He climbed out of the bed and walked to the bathroom. The door shut softly behind him and the shower creaked on.

I pulled the covers up to my chin and sighed. Whatever was between us, it was intense. That much was clear. But the smarter part of me, the careful one who didn't want to be hurt, reminded me:

It had only been *two days.*

In *my* life, two days was *nothing.* Two days could pass before I even *realized* it. Weeks and months became a blur of work, and demands, and anxieties.

Here, two days passed slow and *lingering.* I savored every quiet hour. James had shared a little of the peace he had here.

But look what it had cost him to find it.

He was searching for something. I didn't know if he thought he could find it with me, but I wasn't the answer to his problems. And he wouldn't fix mine. Nothing could be solved in *two days*.

Nothing couldn't become *something* in two days, right?

But maybe, with more time, we could be something else to each other. *Something real.* Maybe I could come back to Colorado sometime. Maybe he could visit me in L.A.

Or maybe I was crazy for imagining any kind of future with him.

The door to the bathroom opened, and he walked out, a cloud of shower steam behind him.

He stared at me, and that burning look was back in his dark, glittering eyes. My doubts began to fade.

Without the long hair, I could see his ears and neck were flushed with heat. The dark hair on his chest and stomach glistened with moisture, and his thick muscles tensed as he looked at me.

And this time, there was no towel to hide *anything*. His cock hung heavy and hard beneath a thatch of dark curls.

It was glorious. To think, I'd had it in my hands the night before. Now I wanted it *inside me*.

I wanted *him*. I wanted to feel his body next to

mine again. I wanted to wrap myself around him and do the things we hadn't done yet. And there was something deeper in my want. I wanted him to feel *safe*. To *trust* me.

I hoped he knew he could.

He climbed onto the bed and crawled over me. "Now," he said, his voice low, "where were we?"

I pulled him closer. "Right here."

Our lips met, and we kissed hungrily. When our tongues touched, I whimpered, and I opened further to him. His tongue filled my mouth, and a low growl escaped him.

He yanked the covers off, and set himself down on top of me, settled between my legs. I ran my hands up and down his back, over the curve of his ass. "Yes," I gasped. "Please."

He licked at my throat, and gripped my hips in his large, rough hands. It felt so good, so natural. It felt like where we were supposed to be.

A noise in the distance broke through the hazy fog of lust. A static buzz, and a feedback whine. He looked up from my throat and over to the radio on his desk.

"White River Dispatch, FA1VV, foxtrot alpha one victor victor, got a way through for you now. Slide's all

clear."

Chapter Thirteen

James

Of course. Brilliant fucking timing.

I looked down at Keeley beneath me. She was so unsure now. She bit her beautiful bottom lip and didn't say a word, but I could see it in her eyes—she was waiting for me to answer. Or to say *something*.

"Shit." That was all I could manage before I rolled away from her and stepped out of the bed. I went to the desk and flicked on the power button on the microphone.

"ADT2B, alpha delta tango two bravo. White River Dispatch, repeat your last message?"

I waited for a response. Keeley rolled over onto her side to face me and leaned on her elbow. Her bangs were askew, and her cheeks blushed coral pink. Her lip was still between her teeth, and her brow furrowed.

I wanted to say *fuck it*, toss the mic onto the ground, turn off the radio and crawl back into that bed with her.

But the radio buzzed again before I let myself do that.

"ADT2B, rockslide on your roadway SE of Baxter is all cleared out. Hell of a mess. You should be good to go."

I sighed. "Copy. Thanks for the update."

"White River out."

I put down the microphone and leaned against the desk.

It might sound ridiculous, but with everything else on my mind, and the beautiful woman I wanted so goddamn bad in front of me... I had forgotten about the fucking rockslide for a while.

I forgot they would clear it by today, and the path out of here would be open.

I forgot she would be leaving. That I said I would take her back to her rental.

My fist clenched. *Son of a bitch. The last thing I want now is to give her up.*

When I brought her here, I hadn't wanted her around. I hadn't wanted *anyone*.

Now I had a way for her to leave, and a reason. The slide was clear. We were no longer *stuck* together.

What happened two days ago seemed so damn far away.

Stuck here together, it seemed like the outside world hadn't existed for a while. Since last night, everything else had faded into background noise.

There was only her, and me, and the way her skin felt against mine. Soft where I was rough, yielding where I was hard.

Like with my art, I took pleasure in the meeting of opposites. With her, the pleasure was *literal*.

"So..." She sat up, pulling the blankets off my bed up to cover her naked body. "The road is clear?"

I nodded. "Yeah." My throat was dry. I felt like I was waking up from a fever dream. A dream where I held on to something I could never have. A dream where my life was different. Where I had other possibilities.

It seemed like she was waiting for me to come back to the bed. When I didn't move, she blinked a few times and turned her eyes away from me.

My damn heart was pounding out of my chest. Maybe it was a mistake even to try something like this. To try to make a stupid dream real.

I had been right that first night, when I backed away from her. Despite how I was starting to feel about my past... I was still the same sorry bastard.

I was pathetic enough that I couldn't just go to her and tell her how I felt.

I couldn't offer Keeley anything beyond what I had. I had nothing—nothing but myself, and all my darkness and clouded past.

It didn't seem like enough for someone like her. Hell, it wasn't *nearly enough*.

The problem was all me. I was feeling things I hadn't felt in years. It was strange to feel good again. To want something more than what little I had in this rustic cabin.

I took a long look at her. Her shiny, dark hair reflected the morning sun, and her long dark lashes brushed her cheeks. She bunched the end of the blankets in her fist and held them close against her chest. Her full lips pouted as she stared out the window.

The part of me that felt good clawed at me from

the inside, demanding that I do what I wanted. What we *both* had wanted just a few minutes ago.

I moved toward the bed, and she stirred, turning toward me.

But I couldn't go back to her. I bent toward the end of the bed and opened a drawer in my dresser. I pulled out a pair of pants and a T-shirt, and I turned my back to her.

All my usual confidence, the typical way I moved through the world these days, alone and detached—something had changed. I didn't know how to act around her now. For her sake, I had to leave her alone.

I had to pretend this was just another fling. That I could take her back to her place, say a quick, cool goodbye, and come home to my silent cabin. *Alone.* Back to *my normal*, however *abnormal* that was. It was what I knew, what I was used to.

I had to pretend that I wouldn't be fighting myself the whole time—that my hands wouldn't be reaching for her uncontrollably, until she was out of my reach.

I tugged on the shirt and stepped into the pants, knowing that if I touched her again, I damn sure wouldn't be able to let her go.

Truth was, I wasn't nearly good enough for

a woman like Keeley Norton. She deserved her city life, her friends, all the creature comforts she didn't have here with me.

"Should probably get you back," I said, rubbing my face with my hands. "I'm sure you want to go home." I sounded empty, and dejected. I couldn't help it. I suppose I was. Even I couldn't lie to myself about that.

With a ragged sigh, I turned back to Keeley.

She looked like she wanted to say something... something angry judging by the way her jaw was set tight. Something told me how confused she was, judging by her wrinkled brow, the way her eyes roamed my face, searching for something that made sense.

Despite all that, she stayed quiet. She tossed back the covers, her beautiful, honey-colored body naked and perfect. Staring at the floor, her eyes narrowed. She reached for her backpack and felt around on the floor for the clothes she had tossed the night before.

And I watched her. It was all I could do to not grab that backpack and toss it out the window. I scratched at my beard and waited.

I had to do what was right for *her*. Even if it hurt like hell.

Chapter Fourteen

Keeley

It was crazy, how everything could change in a moment. How you could get so close to falling off a cliff, and just back away, with the safe, solid ground just a few steps behind you.

I blindly reached for my things, stepping into my shorts and pulling on a discarded flannel shirt. My mind reeled from what had just happened. He'd said no, again, because it was time for me to go.

It was time for both of us to go back to our everyday lives.

But I didn't *want* my everyday life right now. I didn't want *safe* and *solid*. If I did, I wouldn't have even come out to this forest. I wouldn't be sitting *here* right now.

He was slumped against the wall, facing away from me, his hands deep in his pockets. I could see the muscles in his broad back tense beneath the thin T-shirt. *I'm sure you want to go home*, he'd said.

And I did. I had to. There were issues that I needed to work out in my own life.

Just...not yet.

Not without knowing exactly what I was walking away from. Without knowing whether I would ever see him again.

I had to know. *Now or never.*

The distance he was trying to put between us hurt. I wasn't going to lie to myself about that, but James was a master at contradicting his real emotions with his behavior. I had to know if it was that, or he really wanted to get me out of his cabin as quickly as possible now that the slide was cleared.

I hastily buttoned the flannel and zipped my backpack closed with a loud rip. I got up from the bed and walked over to him, right behind him, and reached up to lay my hand on his shoulder.

He turned around to face me. His eyes were tense and sad, searching my face in confusion. The flush was still washing over his skin, and I longed to throw my arms around his neck and pull him back to the bed.

First, though, we needed to talk.

"James."

He didn't say anything. He just stared down at me expectantly, his jaw tight.

I had to get through this quickly. I had to get out whatever I was feeling before my resolve faltered. I took a deep breath and put on my best *getting-shit-done* voice, hoping it would mask how devastated I really felt.

"You asked me if I would ever come back. The thing is... would I be coming back to you? Do you want that?"

"Keeley, wait—"

"Let me finish." I held my hand up and sighed. "I know you've been through a lot. And I'm— I'm still trying to figure out what I want in life. Which is not very fucking easy. None of this is."

He folded his arms across his chest and leaned back against the wall, still silent. *Fine.* I had a lot to say.

"Listen, we live in *very* different worlds. In my world, you don't get anywhere by not going after what you want. You have to make it happen." My heart was pounding. "And you don't get to hide. Like this."

He tilted his head and opened his mouth to speak, but I cut him off.

"I don't blame you for it. I really don't. I'm just telling you why... why I'm doing this." I took a breath and gathered my scattered thoughts.

"What *are* you doing, Keeley?" he asked, in a scratchy, low voice. "You don't even like the life you have. You can find something else. You have other options."

He was right, and that was something I needed to resolve when I got back to Hollywood. I hadn't been happy in a very long time.

Really though, was he talking about getting a life in the city or...

"Do I have the option of having *you* in my life in some way?" I stared deeply into his eyes. "Tell me."

I wondered briefly if he thought he had nothing to offer, this mountain man with a rustic cabin and probably only a few pennies to his name.

Like I gave a damn about *that*? I'd met way too many rich pricks to be at all interested in being with a guy just because of money. All I really

wanted was someone who gave a damn about...
me.

He sighed and shook his head. My heart leaped
into my throat. Was that a *no*, that I didn't have
that option?

He looked somewhere beyond me, into the
distance, thinking.

Dammit! I wasn't going to accept a *no* answer,
not when I knew he was holding back for some
reason. The mysterious connection between us
told me he didn't really want to let this go.

I stepped closer to him and placed my hands
on his chest. My hands slid up to cup his jaw, and
I turned his face to mine. "I'm right here in front
of you," I said firmly. "I'm not whatever is in your
past. I'm the present. And there could be a future
between us."

He blinked at me, his eyes softening.

"I don't know what it looks like," I continued.
"But there's something—*mmm!*"

He shut me up with a hard kiss. His lips closed
over mine and I couldn't say a word. His arms
wrapped around my waist and lifted me up with a
grunt. I tasted him, our tongues brushing against
each other. I whimpered, and he set me down
against the wall.

"Fine." He growled against my neck, his voice shaking. His hot breath gave me chills. "I admit it. This is..." He dragged his lips along my jaw. "This is different. *You're different.*"

His hands brushed up and down my sides as he said gruffly, "I want you." He let out a heaving breath and leaned into me. "More than just now. I want you here with me. I want to wake up with you, wherever you are. I want you again and again. I know the way I feel about you isn't going to go away."

My heart was thundering. I raked my nails softly against his chest and all I could do was nod. *Yes. Me, too. I feel the same way.*

"But I..." He pulled back from me and searched my eyes. "I've been alone a *long* time, Keeley. I don't have anything good to offer you. Just me and this shitty cabin for right now." He swallowed, his mouth a tight line.

Just me. The sadness in his voice gripped my heart. It only made me want him more.

"What makes you think I want anything else?"

His mouth curved in a slow smile.

He took my face in his large, rough hands and pulled me toward him for a soft kiss.

The sharp edges of his beard brushed against my mouth, and I loved the way it felt. I reached for his hips, and the muscles of his torso were hard under my hands.

I gripped the ends of his T-shirt and pulled. "You don't *have* to take me back *yet*... do you?"

He let out an animalistic, feral groan and held me by the shoulders. "I don't want to take you back *at all*."

"That's not what you said two days ago." I couldn't help but tease him.

His nostrils flared and he gave me that wry smile. "Fuck what I said two days ago. I was an asshole."

Then his smile faded, and his arms wrapped tighter around me.

"I really am sorry you got hurt. I never should have sent you off like that."

I laughed and leaned into him. Like it was *his* fault that I'd wandered off track like an idiot because I'd been distracted? Maybe I had wanted to blame that on someone else, but it was all on me. "I think everything worked out okay. So far."

"Yeah, so far..." He pulled me away from the wall. With his arms around me, holding me close, he walked backward toward the bed. He sat down on the mattress and looked up at me.

"I think we were in the middle of something," I said in a sultry voice that I didn't know I had.

I stroked his cheek, his beard rough against my palm, and he nodded.

His hands slid around to my front, and his long fingers picked open the buttons of the shirt I was wearing.

"Hey." He looked up at me. "This is *my* shirt."

I bit my lip. "I know. I was going to steal it."

That wry smile returned. "Hell, you didn't have to steal it. All you had to do was ask. I would have given you any damn thing I have that you want."

"That's no fun," I replied with a smile.

He opened the shirt and leaned forward. "You can keep it." He kissed the skin between my breasts and cupped them in his hands. "And when you wear it... you'll always think of this." His tongue licked up my chest, and he thumbed my hard nipples.

My toes started to curl.

I reached down his back to pull off his T-shirt,

but he wouldn't stop kissing my body, wouldn't move so I could take it off him. I let it go and raked my hands around his waist. When I came to the buttons of his jeans, I undid the top one, and moved my hand lower, stroking his hard cock through his jeans.

He pushed against my palm, and then he moved to my waist and ripped open the button of my shorts. His hand dipped inside, and his fingers found my slick folds. For a moment he felt and stroked me, then he let out a sharp groan.

"Take these off." He tugged at my shorts.

In a tangle of limbs, we helped each other take off all our clothes, and tossed them somewhere on the floor.

We were back to where we started.

He pulled me onto the bed, and rolled over onto his back, dragging me forward by the arm to straddle his thighs.

I ran my trembling hands over his chest, and his stomach. My fingers wound into the dark curls that spread across his body.

He stared at me. It was *that look*, the one that burned so sweetly.

My body caught fire, making *all* of me *burn* for

him.

I moved against him, my soaking wet pussy dragging along his hard length. I shuddered at how good he felt rubbing against me.

He grunted, low and animalistic, and held my hips in his callused hands.

"Fuck," I moaned. *"James..."*

His head fell back, his throat flushed and tense. Then he sat up, his stomach muscles tensed. He pulled me forward and I fell against his shoulder, sighing.

I felt his cock prodding at my entrance, just touching me there, thrusting toward me slowly.

I closed my eyes and panted. I had never wanted any man this badly in my life.

And now I *had* to have him. *All of him.*

He held me steady on his lap as he entered me. He stretched me, and the sweet sting was part of the pleasure.

"Keeley," he rasped. "You're so tight. Fuck! You're.... ahhh...fuck." He groaned as he settled inside me, and I sat fully on his length.

All I could do was rock against him, and hold him close, my fingernails digging into his neck.

We found a slow rhythm, both of us breathing shakily.

He took my face in his hands and looked deeply into my eyes.

"This is what I wanted. This is *all* I wanted. *You*," he said gruffly, his hands stroking down my back.

I kissed him hungrily. "Yes," I moaned, while I thrust against him.

His hand moved down to where our bodies met. His fingers found my clit, and he stroked and circled, the motion tormenting and slow.

"Say you'll come back to me, Keeley." His voice was raspy and guttural. "Tell me."

The feel of him everywhere was so intense. The low rumble of his voice echoed into me.

"I will." My own voice was shaking. "I'll come back to you. Always."

At that moment, I couldn't imagine being with anyone else but him.

He let out a feral sound and thrust faster. I clawed his shoulders because the pleasure was too intense. The muscles in his arms were hard and hot, and his touch on my clit got harder and faster.

I shook and jerked. I was so tense, so damn ready. My breath caught in my throat.

Then it was *too much*. I fell against him, crying out, shivering as the shocks spread through me.

He thrust further, slower. He held me tight until I set my hand on his chest and leaned back, panting.

In my post-orgasmic haze, I realized that he'd wanted to get me off first, watch me as I came apart for him.

The way he looked at me then... it was like he wanted to devour me. Like an animal frenzy deep inside of him was clawing its way out.

He growled, then turned us both over, pressing me into the bed. His large body shadowed mine and being beneath him felt so damn...right.

He sank deep into me, his mouth at my ear. With each rough stroke of his hips, his breath grew harsh, and he snarled and grunted like an out of control beast.

I didn't care, because his ferocity ramped up my own carnal urges.

I matched his rhythm, and every deep movement sent waves of pleasure through me. I couldn't help but moan and whimper, and every sound I made seemed to feed his frenzy. Faster. Deeper. We couldn't seem to get close enough.

His back muscles flexing, he stared down at me, his blue eyes dark and wide, and a choked groan escaped him as he let go, filling me, his breaths short and sharp.

"Fuck! Keeley." The guttural sound of my name coming out of his mouth while he spilled inside me made me realize why he'd wanted to hear me moan his name.

He set me off, and I moaned as I found my own climax, my inner muscles squeezing his cock.

Time seemed to slow. Our frantic heartbeats throbbed against each other, then grew quieter as we lay there together.

He took my face in his hands. His cool lips brushed softly against mine, and his fingers swept the hair from my forehead. "Keeley," he said, low and husky. "I *meant* everything I said."

I sighed and stroked his sweat dampened hair back. "So did I."

And I *had* meant it. I *would* come back to him.

Now, I couldn't imagine just walking away. All I could think about was how I would feel when I got home. How long it would be until I could see him again.

Chapter Fifteen

James

After everything—after we were exhausted from lovemaking, and so hungry we searched through my kitchen to find anything edible—I still had to take Keeley back to her cabin. I didn't want her to spend another night in my crappy place when she was able to get back to hers.

Completely dressed and ready to go, her purple backpack slung behind me, I halted before we walked out the door. I scooped up the carving I'd promised her. "You forgot this." I held it out to her.

She gave me an adorable, exasperated look. "James, I told you I couldn't take it without payment. You do get paid something from your pieces, right?"

I nodded. "Doesn't matter. I want you to have this one, and any other sculptures you like. Every time you see it, maybe it will make you think about me."

Her lips curved up in a smile. "I don't have anything I can give you," she said as she carefully took the piece from my hand.

I shot her an amused grin. "You gave me the best gift I could ever want."

She'd given me her body, and I was pretty sure I'd at least taken a little part of her soul. She'd sure as hell taken *all* of mine.

I watched her blush as she walked outside, so I knew she knew exactly what I was talking about.

I was afraid it would be awkward when I helped her into my beat-up pickup truck and drove the rocky back roads over to where her cabin was situated. I thought maybe there would be an uncomfortable silence. I thought she'd reconsider everything she'd said, that we had done, and she'd already regretted it.

Strange, though—it wasn't awkward at all. Being together in my truck felt natural. It was... fun, actually.

We talked about the forest around us, and what it was like living out here. If only we hadn't been so quiet and hesitant the whole time we were in the damn cabin together. That was my fault. I wanted to make up for that in the future. There was nothing I wanted more than to show Keeley the peace and awe a person could find in the wilderness. The only time it ever got a little rough was when a person was totally alone out here.

Well, I wasn't hesitant anymore about revealing myself to Keeley. I'd give her everything I was and hope that she'd accept it. I'd damn well resolve all the crazy shit in my head and eventually present her with a whole man.

Fuck the "needing time" element of our relationship. Yeah, I needed to clean up the shit show I'd made of my life, but I didn't really need time to know exactly how I felt about Keeley.

I pulled over a couple of times to point out a pretty view, or one of my favorite spots to pick up fallen branches and logs. I never took anything alive to carve into something else. I took whatever was dead and gone, and then tried to bring it back to life. She was interested, and she kept marveling at how beautiful it was here in the Rockies.

Sad, but I guess she'd hardly gotten to see any of it.

I'd make up for *that*, too.

I looked to my right and there she was beside me, gazing out at the forest with a smile, while my truck creaked and rattled. She must have felt me watching her, because she turned to me with that crooked grin I loved.

That smile was so damn sweet that it had melted my stone-cold heart.

She leaned across the old bench seat and kissed me on the cheek.

Damn it. I could feel myself blushing like a fucking teenager. Strangely, I wasn't all that mad about it. I had a feeling that Keeley's open affection would always throw me for a loop.

I wasn't used to it, but that sure as hell didn't mean I didn't like it.

When we found her cabin, I pulled up next to a shiny silver SUV. *Her rental, I guess.* It made my pickup look like it was ready for the junkyard. Truthfully, the truck *was* ready to be ditched for something new. I'd had it since I was a starving artist, before my long stint in the mountains. It worked, and I'd never felt the need to get something else as long as it got me from here to wherever I wanted to go. Until...now. I didn't want Keeley to ride in my creaky old work truck. I'd probably gone nose blind to every nasty scent in the vehicle.

Her rental cabin, if you could really call something that glamorous a cabin, was set against a glen with a killer view of the mountains. It had big picture windows, so I could see right into it, and the inside was as clean and modern as a gallery.

And she'd had to spend the weekend in my dingy cave. I shook my head and opened the rusted truck door to get out.

As I walked around to her door, I started to think. My old cabin and beat up truck—maybe she didn't really mind it all that much. After all, she wanted *me*.

That was a thought that would take some getting used to. She didn't just want to fuck me to find out what I was like, and then leave with a good story. And I didn't want her for one night just to fight off the loneliness.

I wanted *her*, all of her, as *much* and as *often* as I could have her.

Yeah, I got the fact that we had to part ways to figure out our own lives. But I didn't have to fucking *like it.*

I opened her door and held her hand as she stepped out of the truck, and I kept holding it all the way to the entrance of the cabin.

She dug the keys out of her backpack and

unlocked the door. When she pushed it open, a chill escaped from inside. I peeked around the doorframe. It was empty in there, just a couch, a fireplace, a fancy kitchen and some expensive-looking carved tables.

I frowned. *Obviously, the owner is some kind of minimalist.*

I glared at the tables, knowing I could have brought life into them. I could have carved character into those pieces of furniture, so they weren't so damn...cold.

Keeley stepped inside with an exhausted sigh and tossed her backpack on the floor.

I didn't follow her. I stood outside, hands in my pockets, and watched her.

Even in my worn-out old flannel, she fit this place better than I ever could. She was beautiful and intelligent, and she didn't have to prove it with bravado like all the female art dealers I'd screwed before I'd met Keeley.

They were part of my past that I was happy to leave behind.

I stayed outside because I looked at that clean, shiny room, and then down at my old worn boots, caked with mud, and I thought... *That's it, isn't it. A visual metaphor.* I didn't go to art school for nothing.

Whatever decisions I'd come to about my life, I was still a mess. Still a work in progress. It wasn't about the dirty boots. It was me, and my life.

It didn't feel right to muddy things for Keeley, literally or otherwise, by sticking around too long. She said she would come back. I didn't need to hold on so tight, even though I wanted to.

She must have understood my thoughts from the look on my face, because she came back to the door and leaned against the frame with an understanding smile. "You don't want to come in?" she asked softly.

I sighed and shook my head. I hoped she understood me, because words were escaping me at the moment.

She nodded. "Gotta say goodbye eventually. It won't be any easier if we drag it out, right?"

Of course she understood. She didn't have to say it directly, but she got me. And that was worth more than any of my sculptures had ever meant to me.

I'd do *anything* to hold on to that. There wasn't another person on Earth who could understand what was going on in my head.

"No, it won't," I said. "But it's not goodbye. Not really."

She leaned into me and wrapped her arms around my waist. "Not at all."

I felt myself relax at the confidence of her words. I tilted her chin up, and kissed her, slowly, tugging at her lip. I had to savor this one.

But not for too long.

I rested my forehead against hers. "I'll be seeing you," I said hoarsely.

She hummed. "Soon."

She let me go. I walked back to my truck, and it took all my will not to look back, not to throw my resolve to the ground and give in.

I had nearly reached my vehicle when I heard her call out.

"Thank you!"

I had to look back. She was standing in the doorway, smiling and waving, her sweet brown eyes sparkling.

Just like she had when I sent her out to find that fucking trail.

I lifted my hand in acknowledgment and got the hell into my truck before I did something really stupid that would definitely blow our tentative arrangement out of the water.

***

Keeley

I found myself moping around the cabin after James left.

And I *did not* mope. *Ever.* I was always in motion in California, always too busy to think.

Maybe that's the problem.

I'd never had time to think about what I wanted from life because I was too busy handling the one I had.

I stroked a hand down the beautiful sculpture James had given me, feeling the warmth of it beneath my fingers. It was strange that wood could feel so vibrant, but it did, which was a testament to the skill that he had with his art.

The technique is so much like the piece I coveted years ago.

Curious now, I pulled out my laptop and flopped onto the couch. I wasn't sure if I could actually find a catalogue or photos of the old exhibit, but I really wanted to compare James's sculpture to the one I'd wanted to buy when I'd gone to the event.

Do I just think they're similar when they're really not? It's been a long time since I've seen the other piece.

I was grateful that I was currently getting good internet reception, and I started a search by putting the name of the exhibit into the search engine.

I wasn't immediately successful, but one thing led to another until I found an old site that actually still had information posted about that show.

And finally, there it was. I sighed as I saw a picture of that breathtaking piece. I read the brief identification underneath the photo:

Fire and Fury by James Lancaster.

"James? James?" I muttered.

It struck me then that I didn't even know James's *last name.*

I hurriedly carried the computer to the table, gasping as I made the photo larger, and sat it right next to the carving he'd given me.

Even though they were completely different, and brought forth different emotions, I could feel the similarities in the technique.

My pulse kicked up as I started researching the artist behind the Fire and Fury sculpture, my heart telling me something I hadn't been able to recognize before.

It took me a while, but I finally found a short bio for James Lancaster, and discovered that the sculptor lived among the wood he carved, in the Colorado Rocky Mountains.

I closed my laptop.

I didn't really need any further information than that.

Oh, my God, it's him!

"Why?" I uttered softly. "Why wouldn't he *tell* me?"

I felt disappointment and sadness wash over me, and my stomach dropped as I realized James *didn't* entirely trust me.

Even though I hadn't found a picture of James Lancaster, I already knew that the highly sought-after artist and *my James* were one and the same. If I *hadn't* been able to put it together, I would have to be a moron.

It's him. Even if the facts hadn't fallen together so easily, I could feel it in my gut that I was right.

Maybe I'd suspected it the moment I saw his carvings, but the mountain man I knew and the world-renowned artist, James Lancaster, were just too incongruent to meld together as one person in my mind.

What the hell?

The man drove a pickup that was beyond ready for a junkyard.

He lived in a very rustic cabin.

He had none of the necessities that everyone else couldn't live without, like a cell phone and a computer.

Honestly, James lived like a poor hermit, and he seemed perfectly content to live that way.

James *Lancaster* had to be a millionaire many times over.

Not that I minded how James lived if he was happy.

But he wasn't.

He lived that way because he was haunted by his past, not because he *had* to live that way.

He had been giving himself a life he thought he deserved.

"Oh, James," I said in a shaky whisper.

I was hurt because he hadn't told me the truth about who he was.

He'd said that he trusted me.

Now, I just wasn't sure about who he was at all.

Chapter Sixteen

James

I'd only made it halfway back to my cabin before I turned around and drove back to Keeley's place like a man possessed.

She wasn't leaving until tomorrow, and I sure as hell wanted to make use of every second we had.

The moment I pulled back into her place, I sprinted to the door with fear nipping at my heels.

No time to lose.

What if she doesn't come back again?

I need every second I can get to pull her closer to me, so she comes back.

"James? You're here?" Keeley said with a puzzled look on her face as she opened the door.

I walked my muddy boots right into that clean, glassy cabin, wrapped my arms around her waist, and crushed her mouth with mine.

Damned if I care about messing up the pristine cabin floor with my dirty work boots.

Maybe I hadn't wanted this whole situation to get messy because I wasn't into complications.

But for Keeley, I was ready for our relationship to get just as convoluted as it had to be to keep her in my life.

I felt her body tense as I kissed her, even though she responded after a second or two.

I pulled back. "Something's wrong," I surmised as I looked into her dark eyes. Before she could tell me all the reasons why we *shouldn't* be together tonight, I started to speak. "I had to come back. I know it might seem impossible to fall in love with somebody in a matter of a few days. But *I am* in love with you, Keeley. We can take all of this slow and easy. And you don't need to say anything back to me. But I had to tell you how I feel." My tone got huskier as I took her by the shoulders and fell into her eyes. "I'm not letting go this time. Not with you."

She kicked the door closed and turned her back on me as she walked to her couch and picked up her laptop.

I followed her because I couldn't *not* follow her.

She picked her computer up and handed it to me. "This is your piece. Fire and Fury. The sculpture I wanted several years ago but couldn't afford. You're James Lancaster," she said stiffly.

I shrugged, trying to figure out why she'd suddenly went so cold on me. I guess I *hadn't* told her my last name, but did that really matter? I was getting uncomfortable because I was thinking that maybe I shouldn't have just spilled my guts about being in love with her. Maybe it was too soon. "Fire and Fury is mine. I let a dealer have it to put it into an exhibit. It sold. I didn't know it went to California. If you want it, I'll try to track down—"

"That's not the point," she interrupted, her tone so sad that it made my chest ache. "You lied to me, James. You never told me that you were *James Lancaster.*"

I hadn't. She was right. Although I'd never lied, exactly. "Does it matter?" I asked. "And I never lied. I guess I just never mentioned my last name, but was it really that important?"

I put the computer back on the couch. Keeley glared at me, and I suddenly realized I didn't like being the target of her anger very much.

"Of course it matters," she said tightly. "That's one whole portion of your life you didn't share. An important part. Were you afraid I'd go after your money if I knew?"

I scratched at my beard. "It never even entered my mind," I said honestly. "You knew everything that was important. You knew how important my work was to me. You knew my occupation. You just didn't know my last name. Keeley, I told you shit that I'd never share with anybody else. And you're upset because you didn't know my last name?"

She lifted a brow. "Being one of the most renown sculptors in the world isn't important?"

"Not to me," I confessed. "I've never been after the money or the fame. I just wanted to do what I was meant to do. I found out what that was out here in the mountains. I found...part of myself."

She folded her arms across her chest. "You live like a hermit."

I shrugged. "Probably. But I've always had everything I needed. Until I met you, all I was obsessed about was creating my next piece, pouring out my emotions into my sculptures. But that isn't my only purpose anymore. I meant what I said, Keeley. I'm not giving up on us."

"You gave me that piece from your cabin like it was nothing," she said quietly. "It's worth a lot of money."

"It was a damn gift, and it made you happy. If I thought you'd take them, I'd give you every single carving I have at my place just to keep you smiling. Hell, I can make more. I have more money than I can spend in a couple of lifetimes. Why would I need more?" I created because I *had* to, not so I could make more money.

I still sold my work, because if I didn't, I'd run out of space to put my carvings.

I frowned as I saw a tear leak from Keeley's eye because I knew damn well she wasn't the type of woman who cried easily. I hadn't seen a single tear when she'd been hurt and scared after the slide, so that tiny droplet that hit her cheek ripped my heart out.

I had hurt her. I hadn't meant to, but I had. And that nearly destroyed me.

"So you didn't hide the truth?" she asked cautiously as she swept the tear away.

"Hell, no. Why would I? You know the ugly truth about *everything* I've done in my past, and why I'm here."

"You're hiding," she accused.

"Some," I confessed. "But I've pretty much discovered that I belong here, too. Yeah, I need a new truck, and my place could probably use some work."

"Probably?"

"Okay, yeah. It needs a ton of work. But I've always been there alone, and the place is a rental. Nobody ever saw it but me, and I was usually wrapped up in a project."

"And when you're working, you give it everything," she added.

"No reason not to," I said gruffly. "What else did I have?"

"You could have gotten out, met your adoring fans. Honestly, you could have done anything you wanted to do," she pointed out.

I put a hand to the back of my neck to rub out the tenseness there. "Unless you haven't noticed, I'm not exactly a people person."

She snorted. "I noticed."

I was silent for a moment before I said hesitantly, "I never meant to deceive you, Keeley. Since all that other stuff doesn't matter to me, I just never mentioned it. It's not really part of me, if that makes sense. Yeah, I *hear* about my success, but I've never really *seen* it since I don't get out into the world much. It's not real to me."

She stared at me like she was still trying to decide whether or not I was being honest. "Believe me, you *are* famous out there in the art world," she snipped. "You must already know that your sculptures command top dollar."

I shrugged. "I know. I've got the money in the bank, but that's not my definition of success." I hesitated a moment before I asked, "Are you sorry that I came back?"

She was quiet, and the silence stretched out to what seemed like a damn eternity.

Finally, she shook her head. "No. I'm not sorry. I was hurt because I thought you just didn't want to share everything with me. I believe you, James. Although it seems absolutely crazy that you didn't think your fame mattered. I guess I've just spent so much time in Hollywood where name recognition is *everything*, that I never thought about the possibility that it just wasn't important to *you*."

I reached out and swiped a second tear from her face. "Don't cry," I insisted. "*You* matter to me, Keeley. And I haven't cared about anybody for a long time."

I heaved out a sigh of relief as she threw her shapely, warm body into my arms. "You really are crazy, James," she told me again as she hugged me tightly and pressed her body into mine.

I wrapped my arms around her waist and got just as close to her as I possibly could. I could feel my body shudder when I realized she wasn't going to just walk away. "I hope you like lunatics," I grumbled as I swung her into my arms.

I went to the couch and sat down with her sprawled out in my lap.

She swept another tear from her cheek as she smiled. "It seems that I absolutely adore them."

My heart thundered in my chest. I wrapped my arms tighter around her waist, like maybe I was afraid she'd get away. "Enough to be part of my future?"

"Definitely," she confirmed as she rested her forehead against mine. "It might not be an easy relationship with me in Los Angeles and you here right now, but we'll make it work. We have to because—I'm in love with you, too."

"You don't have to say that," I answered hoarsely. *Jesus!* Those words had almost given me a heart attack, but I didn't want her to say them just because I had.

She put a gentle hand in my hair, and I savored the warmth of the simple caress.

"I'm not. I wanted to say it, too, but I was afraid I'd scare you off," she teased. "And I was afraid it was too soon. I'm not the type of woman who just jumps into anything like this, but I'm certain. I came out here to find something, James. The part of me that was missing. And I found...you."

I grunted. "Not exactly what you wanted, probably."

She kept stroking my hair as she replied. "You're what I *needed*. I guess I wasn't searching for *myself*. I was looking for *you*. You're the part of me that was missing. You've taught me how to be still. How to be quiet. How to see things as they really are, and to find peace. I guess I couldn't do that on my own."

Strange as it might seem, I wasn't so sure I hadn't somehow drawn her to me because I needed *her*. "You're an extraordinary woman. You would have eventually figured everything out for yourself." I was thrilled that she thought I'd taught her anything, but I doubted there was much she couldn't do on her own.

Because I couldn't help myself, I grabbed her face in my hands and kissed her. She melted into me so quickly that it made my cock harder than a boulder.

I finally lifted my head and looked at her. *There they were.* Those chocolate brown eyes that made me feel so damn accepted that my fucking chest started to swell. Keeley made me feel human again, like the man I was supposed to be, and I didn't plan on disappointing her in the future by being anyone else.

Sure, I'd still be a crazy artist who got lost in his projects, but with her, I'd be so much more...

Maybe I hadn't *meant* to deceive her, but it was humbling that she'd fallen for me thinking I was just a normal, struggling artist.

"I want to stay with you tonight. I don't want to waste a damn second of the time we have," I grumbled.

"Me, either," she mumbled softly. "I'll cook us some dinner."

"Then you'll never get me to leave," I warned her.

I was grateful that she didn't look worried about having me stay *at all* as she lowered her head to kiss me.

She wants to be with me, stubborn ass and all.

For me, that seemed like a damn miracle, but I

wasn't about to question the best damn thing that ever happened to me.

Tomorrow and the rest of our future would work itself out. I could feel it in my gut.

Right now, I just planned on spoiling her for any other man.

I was going to make *damn sure* she came back to me, over and over again.

Epilogue

Keeley

Summer had come and gone so quickly that it was scary.

The valleys around the Rockies bloomed with wildflowers and weeds, but I knew they'd be gone soon. However, I also knew that when they disappeared, the mountains would bring on something else to marvel over. There were clear skies and strong breezes that blew away the clouds and brought in something new every time I came back to Colorado.

Technically, we were just at the beginning of fall, but the weather had been kind, and it was still warm.

I let out a sigh as I looked at the mountain peaks. My mind quieted, and all I could feel was a sense of peace and happiness because I was back where I belonged. I'd fallen in love with Colorado, these mountains, this place, and I felt a sense of relief that I'd left the city behind me.

I pulled my small four-wheel drive SUV into the driveway of the beautiful cabin that had once seemed like a death sentence to me.

Now, it was *home.*

As soon as the place I'd stayed in on my very first visit to Colorado had come up for sale, James had instantly bought it. It tugged at my heart that I knew he'd done it *for me.* If he'd still been alone, I doubted that he'd have bothered to upgrade.

We'd gotten the pristine cabin messy together and had enjoyed every moment of it, filling it with memories, pictures, James's art, and stuff that would always remind us of how good our life was together.

James and I had made the place *ours*, and we already had so many good memories of the last six months or so that we'd spent together in our new home that my heart pounded with excitement as my vehicle came to a stop.

God, I'd missed James so damn much.

Granted, I'd seen him just a few weeks ago in Los Angeles, but I felt like he took another piece of my soul every time we had to separate.

I smiled at the shiny new pickup in the driveway. James said he'd only bought it because he didn't think I deserved to be riding around in his clunker.

I sighed as I gathered up my stuff from the car. The guy was so damn indulgent when it came to me that it was almost ridiculous. But that was James; he was always ready to give me anything and everything I wanted.

I was still trying to convince him that all I really wanted was...him.

Over the last several months, I'd discovered that the money and his fame really *didn't* mean anything to him. They were just a byproduct of his career. His passion. He payed very little attention to how much money he was making, or how people on the outside praised his work.

Simply put, he didn't give a damn what other people thought. And I actually loved that about him.

I yanked my suitcase from the car, not surprised that James wasn't here to do it for me. I was really early. He wouldn't be expecting me for hours, but I'd moved my ass to get here faster because I missed him.

Not that we hadn't spent a lot of time together; him visiting California, and me returning to Colorado. But it was *never* enough.

I'll never have to leave again. I'm here to stay. Thank God.

James and I had taken our time, both of us figuring out exactly what we wanted. He'd wanted to prove that I didn't need to fix him. That he could resolve his issues. And he had. Splendidly.

He'd found his sister, Olivia, living in California. It turned out that *she'd* been trying to find *him* for a long time. His sister had kicked the abusive asshole to the curb years earlier, and she finally understood why James had tried so hard to protect her. I had to admit, seeing the two of them together again had brought tears of joy to my eyes. As it turned out, James had a nephew, and I doubted if anybody could find a prouder uncle. He spoiled the little boy shamelessly—no matter how much Liv asked him not to.

Olivia had gone back to making pastries in California, and I knew that James was doing his best to try to talk her into making a move to Aspen to open her own shop.

He wanted to fund her whole operation.

Liv was determined that he wouldn't.

I smiled as I entered the house, wondering how long before she'd give into James's not-so-subtle pressure to move here. I was pretty certain it wouldn't be long since he could be incredibly persuasive when he wanted to be.

The house was quiet as I entered and put my stuff down on the floor.

My heart skittered as I looked at the kitchen counter.

James *still* loved his postcards, and they were spread out on the granite surface like somebody had been looking at them just this morning.

I gingerly touched the ones I'd sent him from California. The minute he left me there to return to the mountains, I'd run out and found a postcard for every place we'd visited together and sent them to him in Colorado. Maybe it was kind of sappy that I sent him postcards of every memory we'd made, but he didn't seem to mind. In fact, he apparently treasured every one of them since the majority of them were beaten up like he'd looked at them over and over.

I turned one of them over, already knowing what I'd find since I'd written them.

I miss you.

Three little words, but they'd come from

my heart every single time. The minute we'd separated, my heart had always ached like part of it was missing when he wasn't with me.

Maybe the separations had been necessary because I'd pulled my life together, too, and wrapped up everything in California so I could leave on a high note.

I put my purse on the counter and started looking around the cabin, but to my disappointment, James wasn't anywhere to be found.

I stepped outside, and there was his carving table with his latest piece. It was a tall, curvy block of golden wood. The smooth lines he was finding in the grain twisted lusciously. My eyes followed their path, and they wound and curved across the soft surface.

Gorgeous.

James had mentioned that he'd been working on something that reminded him of me, and strangely, I could feel the heartwarming pull toward the sculpture, *knowing* it was all about us.

Closing the door behind me, I started toward the woods. I pretty much knew where he was if he wasn't inside or working on a sculpture.

Turned out, there was a beautiful pond near this house, just like the one near his old cabin.

We'd spent hours there just watching the wildlife, being still and quiet, wrapped up in each other. It was a special place, the location where he'd asked me to marry him the last time we were here at the cabin together.

Of course, I'd said *yes*—because we were *both ready*. There had been nothing standing in our way anymore.

Not his issues.

Or mine.

Maybe we'd needed that time to work things out by ourselves, but we were both getting damn tired of having to say goodbye.

Never again!

I was enrolled in a cooking school in Aspen, and I was about to pursue my love of all things culinary.

I'd given my work plenty of notice, and although I was going to miss Yasmine and my other friends, I decided I *was not* going to miss my job.

My breath caught as I got to the edge of the clearing with the sparkling pond.

My heart tripped as I saw James sitting next to the water, drinking a mug of coffee, his expression looking like he was far away.

God, he's so beautiful.

The man was as big and as bold as the pieces he made, and just as magnetic.

He must have heard the rustle of my footsteps because he turned as I moved toward him, and my heart soared as those panty-melting blue eyes became laser-focused on me. He looked like a predator who had just spotted some very tasty prey.

He stared at me like I was all he needed.

Everything he wanted.

"You lost?" he called out roughly, his voice cracking just a little, even though I knew he was trying to be nonchalant, mimicking the very first time we met.

You lost? Oh, hell no. Not anymore. He'd found me.

I smiled at him. "Not anymore, handsome," I yelled back.

He put his mug aside as I sprinted toward him.

I flung myself into his arms before he could stand up, landing solidly in his lap.

He was so damn warm, so solid, and totally... mine.

He was quick to put those powerful arms

around me like he'd never let me go. So eager to kiss me that my lips were already parted as his mouth crashed down on mine.

I savored the feel of him, the taste of him, and that masculine pine, mountain-man scent that always drove me crazy.

The embrace was deep and wet, and so intense that molten heat flooded between my thighs. His hands ran up and down my back like he was still trying to convince himself that I was in his arms.

When we surfaced, I pulled back and saw him grinning at me as he said, "You're early."

"You complaining about that?" I teased.

He shook his head and continued to grin.

God, I love that smile.

"Welcome home," he said huskily against the sensitive skin of my neck, a sound that vibrated through my entire being. "I would have been back in the cabin if I'd known you'd show up early. God, I've missed you so damn much, Keeley."

He rolled me down to the ground, and settled himself on top of me, between my legs.

He kissed at my throat, and then moved down my body, unbuttoning my shirt, dragging his beard across my skin. He dug into the cut-off shorts I was wearing, pulling them open, and dragging them down my legs. His lips found the inside of my thigh, and he started kissing farther up, until he reached the spot that never failed to make me gasp and moan.

"James." His name came from my lips with a sigh.

"You're never leaving me again, Keeley. I can't take it one more time. I'm done with that shit," he said gutturally.

My body tensed as he continued to devour every inch of skin he could find.

"I'm never leaving again," I promised in a tremulous voice. "You're stuck with me."

"Thank fuck!" he growled as his big hands cupped my ass.

I let out a sound that was a combination of a laugh and a moan.

We had plenty to talk about, but we'd get to that later.

Much later.

I shivered as James got closer to my slick heat with his wicked mouth.

Maybe my mountain man was a guy of few

words when his sensual hunger overrode any other priorities, but I would never want to tame him. He felt too damn good on top of me, and I loved him exactly the way he was.

Right now, we had lost time to make up for, and sometimes conversation *was* highly overrated.

*****The End*****

About the Author

Lane Parker is an alter-ego of J.S. Scott. She got sucked into reading romance since her teenage years. She reads all kinds of romance books, the hotter the better. She writes what she loves, hot happily ever after contemporary romance stories that feature strong women and bossy Alpha Males.

Books by Lane Parker

Dearest Stalker: A Complete Collection

A Christmas Dream

A Valentine's Dream

Lost: A Mountain Man Rescue Romance

Made in the USA
Columbia, SC
25 November 2024

47525635R00126